Thomas Middleton and Thomas Dekker's The Roaring Girl: A Retelling

David Bruce

Published by David Bruce, 2023.

THOMAS MIDDLETON AND THOMAS DEKKER'S THE ROARING GIRL: A RETELLING

First edition. June 5, 2023.

Copyright © 2023 David Bruce.

ISBN: 979-8223556886

Written by David Bruce.

Table of Contents

CAST OF CHARACTERS..1
PROLOGUE...5
CHAPTER 1 | — 1.1 —...7
— 1.2 —.. 13
CHAPTER 2 | — 2.1 —... 28
— 2.2 —.. 53
CHAPTER 3 | — 3.1 —... 65
— 3.2 —.. 76
— 3.3 —.. 92
CHAPTER 4 | — 4.1 —... 106
— 4.2 —.. 120
CHAPTER 5 | — 5.1 —... 141
— 5.2 —.. 161
EPILOGUE 177
APPENDIX A: NOTES | — Elizabethan Betrothals — 179
ANECDOTES | — 2.2 —... 181
— 3.1 —... 182
— 4.2 —... 183
— 5.1 —... 184
— 3.1 —... 185
— 5.1 —... 186
— EPILOGUE — 187
APPENDIX B: FAIR USE... 188
APPENDIX C: ABOUT THE AUTHOR.. 189
APPENDIX D: SOME BOOKS BY DAVID BRUCE 190

Dedication

Dedicated to Cliff Craft

On Sunday, 17 May 2007, my friend Cliff Craft died in Athens, Ohio. Most people probably thought of him as a homeless scavenger, but people who knew him realized that he was a generous person. He lived in low-income housing, and he frequently allowed homeless people to stay in his apartment. Because of his illnesses, including epilepsy, he lived on a monthly Social Security check and whatever money he found on his frequent walks around town, but he was generous with the money he had. Each month, he deposited his Social Security check at Hocking Valley Bank, but not all of the money ended up in his own account. According to Hocking Valley Bank branch manager Kim Sparks, for approximately two years before Mr. Craft died, he deposited some of his money each month into an account that had been set up to help a girl who had been injured in an accident. Truly, Mr. Craft's life shows that people don't need to be wealthy to do good deeds.

***

The doing of good deeds is important. As a free person, you can choose to live your life as a good person or as a bad person. To be a good person, do good deeds. To be a bad person, do bad deeds. If you do good deeds, you will become good. If you do bad deeds, you will become bad. To become the person you want to be, act as if you already are that kind of person. Each of us chooses what kind of person we will become. To become a good person, do the things a good person does. To become a bad person, do the things a bad person does. The opportunity to take action to become the kind of person you want to be is yours.

A guru had a disciple to whom he revealed a sacred mantra, along with a warning not to reveal the mantra to anyone. The disciple asked, "What will happen if I reveal the sacred mantra?" The guru replied, "Anyone to whom you reveal the sacred mantra will learn about Ultimate Goodness and will become wiser. But you will be excluded from discipleship." Immediately, the disciple ran to the marketplace and began shouting the sacred mantra to everyone there. The other disciples came to the guru and demanded that the first disciple be excluded from discipleship because he had revealed the sacred mantra. The guru smiled, agreed, and said, "Yes, you are right. He is no longer a disciple. Today, he has become a guru."

Educate Yourself
Read Like A Wolf Eats
Be Excellent to Each Other
Books Then, Books Now, Books Forever

***

In this retelling, as in all my retellings, I have tried to make the work of literature accessible to modern readers who may lack some of the knowledge about mythology, religion, and history that the literary work's contemporary audience had.

Do you know a language other than English? If you do, I give you permission to translate this book, copyright your translation, publish or self-publish it, and keep all the royalties for yourself. (Do give me credit, of course, for the original retelling.)

I would like to see my retellings of classic literature used in schools, so I give permission to the country of Finland (and all other countries) to give copies of this book to all students forever. I also give permission to the state of Texas (and all other states) to give copies of this book to all students forever. I also give permission to all teachers to give copies of this book to all students forever.

Teachers need not actually teach my retellings. Teachers are welcome to give students copies of my books as background material. For example, if they are teaching Homer's *Iliad* and *Odyssey*, teachers are welcome to give students copies of my *Virgil's* Aeneid: *A Retelling in Prose* and tell students, "Here's another ancient epic you may want to read in your spare time."

CAST OF CHARACTERS

SIR ALEXANDER Wengrave.

NEATFOOT, his serving-man. A neat's foot is a cow's foot: an article of food. "Neat foot" can also mean that he is elegantly dressed. His diction is elevated.

SIR ADAM Appleton.

SIR DAVY Dapper.

SIR BEAUTEOUS Ganymede. In mythology, Ganymede was the cupbearer to Jupiter, king of the gods.

SIR THOMAS Long.

LORD NOLAND.

Young SEBASTIAN Wengrave.

JACK Dapper, son to Sir Davy.

GULL, his page. A "gull" is a simpleton who can be duped by a conman or conwoman. A "gull" is gullible.

GOSHAWK. A goshawk is a kind of hawk.

GREENWIT. "Green" means "youthful." A "green wit" is a "naïve intelligence."

LAXTON. His name is "Lacks Stone." He has sold all his land and so he lacks stones in fields. A "stone" is also a slang word for "testicle," and so his name seems to indicate that he is impotent, but he spends money on wenches.

TILTYARD, a feather-seller. A tilt yard is an area for tournaments in which tilts, aka jousts, are held. Feathers are used in arrows, and they are worn by gallants attending tournaments.

MISTRESS TILTYARD. "Mistress" here means "Mrs."

OPENWORK, a sempster. "Sempster" is now used for the masculine form of "seamstress," but at the time of this play, a sempster could be male or female. Sempsters sew and mend clothing. "Openwork" is a piece of cloth with holes that show the material underneath the article of clothing. An example is lace.

MISTRESS Rosamond OPENWORK. "Mistress" here means "Mrs."

GALLIPOT, an apothecary. Hippocrates was an ancient Greek physician. A gallipot was used for medicines. Apothecaries are pharmacists who make medicines.

MISTRESS Prudence GALLIPOT. "Mistress" here means "Mrs."

MOLL Cutpurse, the Roaring Girl. "Moll" is a nickname for "Mary," a name that calls to mind purity. "Moll" also means "whore." Roaring boys were swaggering young men who often fought each other and others.

Ralph TRAPDOOR. In the theater, trapdoors could lead to Hell. Any character named "Trapdoor" is likely to be dangerous.

TEARCAT. To "tear a cat" means to "bluster." Tearcats can be bullies and swaggerers.

SIR GUY Fitzallard.

MARY Fitzallard, his daughter.

CURTILAX, a sergeant. A curtal-ax is a short broadsword or cutlass. Sergeants have the power to arrest offenders.

HANGER, his yeoman (assistant). A hanger is a loop tied to a belt. A rapier or other kind of sword hangs in it.

MINISTRI. Servants. *Ministri* is Latin for "servants."

COACHMAN.

PORTER.

TAILOR.

Gentlemen.

CUTPURSES.

FELLOW.

NOTES:

The subtitle of *The Roaring Girl* is *or Moll Cutpurse*.

People at this time carried their money in a purse, a moneybag tied to their belt with a string. Cutpurses cut the string and stole the bag of money.

The Roaring Girl first appeared in print in 1611.

The Roaring Girl is the final collaboration between Thomas Middleton and Thomas Dekker. Their other two collaborative plays are *The Honest Whore, Part 1* (a city comedy, as is *The Roaring Girl*) and *The Bloody Banquet* (a revenge tragedy).

Roaring boys were bully boys who enjoyed fighting.

The Roaring Girl, Moll Cutpurse, is based on a real person: Mary Frith. The book *The Life and Death of Mrs. Mary Frith, Commonly Called Moll Cutpurse, Exactly Collected and Now Published for the Delight and Recreation of All Merry-Disposed Persons* appeared in 1662.

A woman who was similar to Moll Cutpurse (and Mary Frith) was Meg of Westminster, whose life was written about in *The Life and Pranks of Long Meg of Westminster* (1582).

In this society, a person of higher rank would use "thou," "thee," "thine," and "thy" when referring to a person of lower rank. (These terms were also used affectionately and between equals.) A person of lower rank would use "you" and "your" when referring to a person of higher rank.

"Sirrah" was a title used to address someone of a social rank inferior to the speaker. Friends, however, could use it to refer to each other.

The word "wench" at this time was not necessarily negative. It was often used affectionately.

EDITIONS:

Thomas Middleton and Thomas Dekker. *The Roaring Girl*. Elizabeth Cook, ed. London: A & C Black; New York: W.W. Norton, 1997.

Thomas Middleton and Thomas Dekker. *The Roaring Girl*. Andor Gomme, ed. London: Benn; New York: W. W. Norton, 1976.

Thomas Middleton and Thomas Dekker. *The Roaring Girl*. Paul Mulholland, ed. Manchester; Wolfeboro, New Hampshire, USA: Manchester University Press, 1987.

Thomas Middleton and Thomas Dekker. *The Roaring Girl*. Jennifer Panek, ed. New York, London: W.W. Norton. and Company, 2011.

The Routledge Anthology of Renaissance Drama. Simon Barker and Hilary Hinds, eds. London; New York: Routledge, 2003.

Thomas Middleton and Thomas Dekker. *The Roaring Girl and Other City Comedies*. James Knowles, ed. Oxford, New York: Oxford University Press, 2001.

Plays on Women. Kathleen E. McLuskie and David Bevington. Manchester; New York: Manchester University Press, 1999.

WEBSITES

https://www.luminarium.org/sevenlit/middleton/thomasbib.htm

https://www.luminarium.org/sevenlit/middleton/

AN ONLINE MODERN-LANGUAGE EDITION WITH NOTES BY CHRIS CLEARY

https://tech.org/~cleary/roar.html

A BOOK OF SCOUNDRELS

Charles Whibley (1859-1930). *A Book of Scoundrels.*
Charles Whibley's *A Book of Scoundrels* contains a chapter on Moll
Cutpurse and Jonathan Wild. It is available on Gutenberg:
https://www.gutenberg.org/ebooks/1632

PROLOGUE

The Prologue appeared and said to you, the audience members and readers:

"A play expected long [long expected] makes the audience look

"For wonders, that each scene should be a book,

"Compos'd to all perfection; each one [each audience member] comes

"And brings a play in's [in his] head with him: up he sums

"What he would of a roaring girl have writ [written];

"If that he finds not here, he mews at it."

Audience members could insult a play by mewing like a cat at it.

The Prologue continued:

"Only we entreat you think our scene

"Cannot speak high, the subject being but mean."

This play is not high tragedy, but rather mean — low — comedy.

The Prologue continued:

"A roaring girl whose notes till now never were [heard in the theater]

"Shall fill with laughter our vast theatre."

The Roaring Girl was first performed at the Fortune Theatre on Golden Lane in Cripplegate.

The Prologue continued:

"That's all which I dare promise: tragic passion,

"And such grave stuff, is this day out of fashion.

"I see attention sets wide ope [open] her gates

"Of hearing, and with covetous [eager] list'ning waits,

"To know what girl this roaring girl should be,

"For of that tribe are many. One is she

"That [Who] roars at midnight in deep tavern bowls [drinking vessels],

"That [Who] beats the watch [watchman or watchmen], and constables controls [rebukes constables];

"Another roars i' th' daytime, swears, stabs, gives braves [tries to start fights],

"Yet sells her soul to the lust of fools and slaves.

"Both of these are suburb roarers."

Suburb roarers are members of the lower class in the suburbs of London.

The Prologue continued:

"Then there's beside

"A civil city roaring girl, whose pride,

"Feasting, and riding, shakes her husband's state [estate and wealth],

"And leaves him roaring [begging for food or money] through an iron grate."

The iron grate is that of a debtors' prison.

The Prologue continued:

"None of these roaring girls is ours: she flies

"With wings more lofty. Thus her character lies;

"Yet what need characters, when to give a guess

"Is better than the person to express?

"But would you know who 'tis? Would you hear her name?

"She is call'd mad Moll; her life, our acts proclaim."

CHAPTER 1

— 1.1 —

Mary Fitzallard, who was disguised as a seamstress carrying a box for bands (collars), and Neatfoot, a serving-man, met and talked together in Sebastian's chambers in Sir Alexander's house.

Mary Fitzallard was the daughter of Sir Guy Fitzallard.

Neatfoot, a serving-man of Sir Alexander Wengrave, had a napkin on his shoulder and a plate in his hand. He had just come away from a dining table at which he was serving Sebastian Wengrave, the son of Sir Alexander Wengrave. Now he was here to find what the disguised Mary Fitzallard wanted.

Neatfoot, whose diction was elevated, said to her, "Sweet damsel emblem of fragility, is it into the ears of the young gentleman our young master, Sir Alexander's son, that you desire to have a message transported, or do you prefer to be transcendent?"

The word "transcendent" meant "rise to his level," by being allowed to give her message to Sebastian in person. The word can also be used to refer to the rising of a pregnant belly.

"I desire a private word or two, sir," the disguised Mary Fitzallard said. "Nothing else."

Neatfoot said, "You shall fructify in that which you come for: Your pleasure shall be satisfied to your full contentation. I will, fairest tree of generation, watch when our young master is erected, that is to say, up, and deliver him to this your most white hand.

The word "fructify" means 1) become fruitful, and/or 2) become pregnant.

"Pleasure" can mean sexual pleasure.

The word "erected" means "stands up after dining," but it can also refer to an erect penis.

A "white hand" is 1) elegant handwriting, and/or 2) an elegant hand. White hands are unused to laboring outside and so are not tanned.

This society preferred light skin to dark skin.

"Thanks, sir," the disguised Mary Fitzallard said.

Neatfoot said, "And moreover I will certify — that is, inform — him that I have culled out for him, now his belly is replenished, a daintier bit or modicum than any that lay upon his trencher at dinner, the midday meal. Has he notion of your name, I beseech your chastity?"

"I am one, sir, of whom he bespake — placed an order for — falling bands," the disguised Mary Fitzallard said.

"Falling bands" was a new fashion: falling ruffs. They fell flat around the neck rather than stiffly sticking out.

Neatfoot said, "Falling bands. It shall so be given — reported — to him. If you please to venture your modesty in the hall among a curly-headed company of rude serving-men, and take such as they can set before you, you shall be most seriously and ingenuously welcome."

"Rude" can mean 1) unmannerly, or 2) unsophisticated.

"Well come" can mean "achieve sexual orgasm."

"I have dined indeed already, sir," the disguised Mary Fitzallard said.

Neatfoot said, "Or will you vouchsafe to kiss the lip of a cup of rich Orleans in the buttery among our waiting-women?"

Orleans wine was from the Loire region in France.

A buttery was a storage area for liquors.

"Not now, indeed, sir," the disguised Mary Fitzallard said.

Neatfoot said, "Our young master shall then have a feeling — a sense — of your being here. Presently — immediately — it shall so be given to him."

The disguised Mary Fitzallard said:

"I humbly thank you, sir."

Neatfoot exited.

The disguised Mary Fitzallard said to herself:

"Except that my bosom is full of bitter sorrows, I could smile to see this formal ape play antic, mad, grotesque tricks.

"But in my breast a poisoned arrow sticks, and smiles cannot become me."

Pretending to be talking to Sebastian, the disguised Mary Fitzallard said:

"Love woven slightly and slackly, such as thy false heart makes, wears out as lightly, but love being truly bred in the soul like mine bleeds even to death at the least wound it takes.

"The more we quench this fire, the less it slakes.

"Oh, me!"

Sebastian Wengrave entered the room with Neatfoot.

"A sempster wants to speak with me, do thou say?" Sebastian said to Neatfoot.

"Yes, sir, she's there, *viva voce*, to deliver her auricular confession," Neatfoot said.

Auricular confessions were delivered to priests. Often, priests heard confessions of sexual misdeeds.

Viva voce is Latin for "by word of mouth."

Sebastian said to the disguised Mary Fitzallard, "With me, sweet heart? What is it?"

"I have brought home your bands, sir," the disguised Mary Fitzallard said.

"Bands" are "collars and ruffs."

Sebastian asked:

"Bands?"

He then said:

"Neatfoot."

"Sir," Neatfoot said.

"Please look into the dining room, for all the gentlemen are close to rising from the table," Sebastian ordered.

"Yes, sir, a most methodical attendance shall be given," Neatfoot said.

"And do thou hear me?" Sebastian said. "If my father should call for me, say that I am busy with a sempster."

"Yes, sir, he shall know that you are busied with a needlewoman," Neatfoot said.

The slang meaning of "needle" is "penis."

The slang meaning of "needlewoman" is "harlot."

"Say it in his ear, good Neatfoot," Sebastian said.

Sebastian did not want people to know that he was alone with the woman.

"It shall be so given to him," Neatfoot said.

He exited.

"Bands?" Sebastian said, not recognizing the disguised Mary Fitzallard. "You are mistaken, sweet heart, I ordered none. When, where? I ask, what bands? Let me see them."

The disguised Mary Fitzallard replied:

"Yes, sir, a bond fast sealed with solemn oaths, subscribed unto as I thought with your soul, delivered as your deed in sight of heaven.

"Is this bond cancelled? Have you forgotten me?"

She removed her disguise.

Recognizing her, Sebastian said:

"Ha! Life of my life! Sir Guy Fitzallard's daughter!

"What has transformed my love to this strange shape?"

He said to himself:

"Wait, make all sure and secure."

He locked the door and then said:

"So, now speak and be brief because the wolf's at door that lies in wait to prey upon us both: Danger is near. Although my eyes are blessed by seeing your eyes, yet this so-strange disguise you were wearing fills me with fear and wonder."

"Mine's a loathed sight: I am loathsome to look at," Mary Fitzallard said. "Otherwise, why are you banished so long from the sight of me?"

Sebastian said:

"I must cut short my speech. In broken language, I can say thus much:

"Sweet Moll, I must shun thy company."

"Moll" is a nickname for "Mary."

Sebastian continued:

"I court another Moll. My thoughts must run as a horse runs that's blind round in a mill, out every step yet keeping one path still."

In other words, he will be like a blindfolded horse that is out — at a distance from a central point —as it walked in a circle and turned a millstone.

Sebastian was saying that he will often appear to be unfaithful to Mary, but in reality he will be faithful to her. He will seem to be far from the central goal — marriage to Mary — but the path he follows, although circuitous, will achieve that goal.

Mary Fitzallard said:

"Umm! Must you shun my company? In one knot both our hands by the hands of heaven have been tied. Is it now to be broken? I thought myself once your bride."

Sebastian and Mary had agreed to marry each other, and their fathers had witnessed the agreement, but a problem had arisen.

Mary Fitzallard continued:

"Our fathers did agree on the time when, and must another bedfellow fill my room?"

Her "room" is her vagina. She wanted to marry Sebastian, but now it appeared that she might have to marry another man.

Sebastian said:

"Sweet maiden, let's lose no time. It is in heaven's book set down that I must have thee. An oath we took to keep our vows, but when the knight your father was from my father departed, storms began to sit upon my covetous father's brows, which fell from them on me. He reckoned up what gold this marriage would draw from him, at which he swore that to lose so much blood could not grieve him more."

Sebastian's father, Sir Alexander, had agreed to give Sebastian some lands when he married Mary.

Sebastian continued:

"He then tried to dissuade me from marrying thee; he called thee not fair and beautiful, and he asked what is she but a beggar's heir?

"He scorned thy dowry of five thousand marks."

"Marks" are units of money. One mark is two-thirds of one pound.

Sebastian continued:

"If such a sum of money could be found, and if I would marry you with that, he'd not undo it, provided his moneybags might add nothing to it, but he vowed, if I took thee, nay, more, he did swear it, I should inherit from him nothing save birth."

If Mary's father will pay the dowry of five thousand marks, Sebastian's father will not prevent the marriage, but he will give Sebastian nothing. In fact, Sebastian will inherit nothing from him except his family name.

Five thousand marks are £3,333 (Great Britain pounds).

As is usual in romantic comedy, Sebastian's father was being unreasonable.

"What follows then? My shipwreck — my ruin?" Mary Fitzallard asked.

Sebastian said:

"Dearest, no. Although wildly in a labyrinth I go, my end is to meet thee. With a side wind I must now sail, else I no haven can find but both must sink forever.

"There's a wench called Moll, mad Moll or merry Moll, a creature so strange in quality that a whole city takes note of her name and person. All that affection I owe to thee I spend on her in counterfeit passion to madden my father.

"He believes that I dote upon this roaring girl, and he grieves as it becomes a father for a son who could be so bewitched.

"Yet I'll go on this crooked way, sigh always for her, feign dreams in which I'll talk only of her. These streams shall, I hope, force my father to consent that here with you I anchor rather than be rent and torn apart upon a rock so dangerous.

"Are thou pleased, because thou see we are waylaid, that I take a path that's safe, although it is far about?"

"May my prayers with heaven guide thee," Mary Fitzallard said.

Sebastian said:

"Then I will continue on.

"My father is at hand. Kiss me and be gone.

"Hours shall be watched for meetings: We will find times to meet. I must now ...

"As men for fear, to a strange idol bow."

Mary Fitzallard kissed him and said, "Farewell."

Sebastian said:

"I'll guide thee forth; when next we meet

"A story about Moll shall make our mirth more sweet."

They exited.

— 1.2 —

Sir Alexander Wengrave, Sir Davy Dapper, Sir Adam Appleton, Goshawk, Laxton, and some gentlemen talked together in the parlor of Sir Alexander's house.

Sir Alexander Wengrave was the father of Sebastian Wengrave, who was in love with Mary Fitzallard.

"Thanks, good Sir Alexander, for our bounteous cheer," one of the gentlemen said.

"Cheer" is food and drink.

"Bah, bah, in giving thanks you pay too dear," Sir Alexander said.

"When bounty spreads the table, truly, it would be a sin, at leave-taking, if thanks should not step in," Sir Davy Dapper said.

"No more of thanks, no more," Sir Alexander said. "Aye, by the Virgin Mary, sir, the inner room was too close and stuffy. How do you like this parlor, gentlemen?"

"Oh, surpassingly well!" one of the gentlemen said.

"What a sweet breath the air casts here, so cool!" Sir Adam said.

"I like the view best," Goshawk said.

"See how it is furnished," Laxton said.

"A very fair, sweet room," Sir Davy Dapper said.

Sir Alexander said:

"Sir Davy Dapper, the furniture and paintings that adorn this room cost many a fair grey groat before they came here, but good things are most cheap when they are most dear."

A groat is a small amount of money, but Sir Alexander was boasting that he had spent much money on his household furnishings. He knew that spending money on high-quality items rather than cheaping out on low-quality items is less expensive in the long run.

A person who buys one pair of good, although expensive, boots will have dry feet for years. A person who frequently buys cheap, bad boots will spend more money in the long run and will sometimes have wet feet.

Sir Alexander continued:

13

"When you look into my galleries and see how splendidly they are trimmed up and decorated, you all shall swear that you are highly pleased to see what's set down there: stories of men and women mixed together, fair ones with foul, like sunshine in wet weather.

"Within one square — one room — a thousand heads are laid so closely together that the room appears to be made entirely of heads."

The walls of Sir Alexander's galleries are crowded with portraits closely placed together.

Sir Alexander continued:

"As many faces there filled with blithe looks show like the promising titles of new books written merrily, the readers being their own eyes, which seem to move and to give plaudities: applause.

"And here and there, while thronged heaps and multitudes do listen with obsequious — that is, dutiful — ears, a cutpurse thrusts and leers with hawk's eyes for his prey. I need not show him to you. By his hanging — gloomy and fit to be hanged and hanging in a portrait — villainous look, you yourselves may know him — the face is drawn so rarely and splendidly.

"Then, sir, below, the very flower as it were waves to and fro, and like a floating island seems to move upon a sea bound in with shores above."

Sir Alexander's galleries were the spectators of the play he was acting in. The stage was like an island in the midst of the spectators on three sides. Cutpurses — pickpockets — sometimes plied their trade in the audience.

Sebastian and Master Greenwit entered the scene and listened.

"These sights are excellent," one of the gentlemen said.

"I'll show you all of them," Sir Alexander said. "Since we are met, let's make our parting cheerful."

"This gentleman, my friend Greenwit, will take his leave, sir," Sebastian said to his father, Sir Alexander.

"Take his leave, Sebastian?" Sir Alexander said. "Who?"

"This gentleman," Sebastian said, indicating Greenwit.

Sir Alexander said to Greenwit, "Your love and courtesy, sir, has already given me some time, and if you please to trust my age and indulge an old man — me — with more, it shall pay double interest. Good sir, stay."

"I have been too bold," Greenwit said.

He did not want to outstay his welcome.

Sir Alexander replied:

"Not so, sir. A merry day among friends being spent is better than gold saved."

He then said:

"Some wine, some wine. Where are these knaves — these servants — I employ?"

Neatfoot and three or four serving-men entered the scene.

"At your worshipful elbow, sir," Neatfoot said.

"You are kissing my maids, drinking, or fast asleep," Sir Alexander said.

"Your worship has described us correctly," Neatfoot said.

Sir Alexander said to the servants:

"You varlets, move quickly! Bring chairs, stools, and cushions!"

The servants brought the items into the room.

Sir Alexander said:

"Please, Sir Davy Dapper, make that chair thine."

"It is but an easy gift, and yet I thank you for it, sir," Sir Davy Dapper said. "I'll take it."

It was an easy chair: a chair that gave ease.

In this society, stools were common items of furniture. Higher-ranking guests would be offered chairs with backs.

"Here's a chair for old Sir Adam Appleton," Sir Alexander said.

"It's a back friend to your worship," Neatfoot said to old Sir Adam Appleton.

A "back friend" is a friend who is a supporter. A back friend can also be a chair with a back. Back friends, however, can also be false friends: people who are secret enemies to you.

Sir Adam Appleton said, "By the Virgin Mary, good Neatfoot, I thank thee for it. Back friends sometimes are good."

"Please make that stool your perch, good Master Goshawk," Sir Alexander said.

Sitting down, Goshawk said, "I stoop to your lure, sir."

A hawk would stoop — that is, swoop — to a lure while being trained. The lure was a fake bird.

A goshawk is a kind of hawk.

Sir Alexander then said, "Son Sebastian, take Master Greenwit to a stool beside you."

"Sit, dear friend," Sebastian said to Greenwit.

Sir Alexander said to Laxton, who was still standing:

"Master Laxton."

He then ordered the servants:

"Furnish Master Laxton with what he lacks, a stone — a stool I should say, a stool."

"Laxton" means "lacks stone." In the slang of the time, a "stone" is a testicle.

"I would rather stand, sir," Laxton said.

In the slang of the time, a "stand" is a penile erection.

Sir Alexander replied:

"I know you would, good Master Laxton."

He dismissed the servants by saying, "So, so."

The servants exited.

Sir Alexander then said:

"Now here's a mess of friends."

A mess of friends is a group of four friends. The four friends were Sir Alexander, Sir Davy Dapper, Sir Adam Appleton, and Master Laxton.

Sebastian and Greenwit were seated a short distance away from the older men.

Sir Alexander then said:

"And, gentlemen, because time's hourglass shall not be running long, I'll quicken it with a pretty tale."

In other words: He would make time pass quickly by telling his friends a story.

"Good tales do well in these bad days, where vice does so excel," Sir Davy Dapper said.

"Begin, Sir Alexander," Sir Adam Appleton requested.

Sir Alexander said, "Yesterday I met an aged man upon whose head was scored a debt of just so many years as these that I owe to my grave: the man you all know."

The aged man was as old as Sir Alexander himself.

The "scored" head was a face and neck with wrinkles.

One of the gentlemen said, "Please tell us his name, sir."

Sir Alexander said:

"Nay, you shall pardon me for not telling you.

"But when he saw me, he gave a sigh that broke, or seemed to break, his heartstrings."

This society believed that the heart was supported by strings that could break when a person was stressed.

Sir Alexander continued:

"Thus he spoke:

"'Oh, my good knight,' says he, and then his eyes were richer even by that which made them poor — and pour. They had spent so many tears they had no more."

According to the *Oxford English Dictionary*, one meaning of "rich" as applied to color is "strong, deep, warm."

The old man's eyes were red from crying.

Also according to the *Oxford English Dictionary*, "Rich" can be used to describe an inflamed and reddened nose or face.

Sir Alexander continued:

"'Oh, sir,' says he, 'you know it, for you have seen blessings to rain upon my house and me.

"'Fortune, who enslaves men, was my slave; her wheel has spun me golden threads, for, I thank heaven, I never had but one cause to curse my stars.'"

Lady Fortune is a goddess who doles out good fortune and bad fortune. Lady Fortune had a wheel of fortune that turned, causing good fortune to turn to bad, and vice versa, while the Fates had a spinning wheel that spun the thread of life for individual human beings.

Sir Alexander continued:

"I asked him then what that one cause might be."

One of the gentlemen asked, "So, what was it, sir?"

Sir Alexander said:

"He paused.

"We often see a sea so much becalmed there can be found no wrinkle on the sea's brow, the sea's waves being drowned in their own rage, but when the imperious winds use strange invisible tyranny to shake both heaven's and earth's foundation at their noise, the seas, swelling with wrath to impart that fray caused by the winds, rise up and are wilder, and madder, than the winds."

The sea had been rough, but the roughness had subsided as if the waves had been drowned and so were quiet. But then an outside source of roughness — strong winds — arose and imparted roughness to the waves, which became rougher than the winds.

First is the calm, and then is the storm.

Sir Alexander continued:

"Even like that this good old man was by my question stirred up to roughness. You might see his gall — his bitterness — flow even in his eyes. Then he grew fantastical and bizarre in his behavior."

"Fantastical?" Sir Davy Dapper said.

He laughed.

"Yes, and he talked oddly," Sir Alexander said.

"Please, sir, proceed," Sir Adam said. "How did this old man end and conclude?"

Sir Alexander said:

"By the Virgin Mary, sir, thus: He left his wild fit to read over his cards."

The aged man metaphorically looked over the cards that Lady Fortune had dealt him, and he realized that his hand was a good one.

Sir Alexander continued:

"Yet then, though age cast snow on all his hairs, he rejoiced because, says he, 'The god of gold has been to me no niggard: that disease from which all old men sicken, avarice, never infected me.'"

"He does not mean himself, I'm sure," Laxton said to himself.

Sir Alexander continued his story:

"The old man says, 'For, like a lamp fed with continual and inexhaustible oil, I spend and throw my light to all who need it, yet I have still enough to serve myself. Oh, but,' says he, 'although Heaven's dew falls thus on this aged tree, I have a son who like a wedge cleaves my very heart-root.'"

The "heart-root" is the center of the deepest emotions.

"Had he such a son?" Sir Davy Dapper asked.

Sebastian said to himself, "Now I smell a fox strongly."

Foxes are known for being crafty; a fox is also a type of sword.

Sebastian suspected that his father was about to talk about him.

Sir Alexander said, "Let's see. No, Master Greenwit is not yet so mellow in years as the old man's son; but the old man's son is as like Sebastian, just like my son Sebastian, as to be such another."

Sebastian said to himself, "How finely like a fencer my father fetches his by-blows — his side strokes — to hit me, but if I don't beat you at your own weapon of subtlety and guile …."

Sebastian now knew that Sir Alexander's story was about the two of them.

"Your own weapon" is "the weapon you are most expert in."

Sir Alexander continued the old man's story:

"'This son,' said he, 'who should be the column and main arch to my house, the crutch to my age, becomes a whirlwind shaking the firm foundation.'"

"He is some prodigal," Sir Adam said.

The parable of the Prodigal Son is told in Luke 15:11-32.

Sebastian said to himself about Sir Adam, "Well shot, old Adam Bell!"

Adam Bell was a famous archer.

Sir Alexander continued the old man's story:

"'He is no city monster neither, no prodigal, but he is sparing, wary, civil, and, although wifeless, an excellent husband — a thrifty head of household — and such a traveler, he has more tongues in his head than some have teeth.'"

"Tongues" are languages, but a person with a double tongue is deceitful.

"I have only two teeth in my head," Sir Davy Dapper said.

"So sparing and so wary?" Goshawk said. "What then could so vex his father?"

"Oh, a woman!" Sir Alexander said.

"A flesh-fly — that can vex any man," Sebastian said.

A flesh-fly is a fly that deposits its eggs in rotting flesh.

Sir Alexander said:

"A scurvy, worthless woman, on whom the passionate old man swore his son doted. 'A creature,' says he, 'that nature has brought forth to mock the sex of woman.' It is a thing one does not know how to name; her birth began before she was all made — and all maiden. It is woman more than man, man more than woman, and, which to none can happen, the sun gives her two shadows to one shape."

Sir Alexander was talking about Moll Cutpurse, who behaved in some ways like a man. He believed that she was born before acquiring all the qualities of a woman, thus causing her masculine traits. The two shadows, both of which were hers, were those of a man and of a woman.

Sir Alexander continued:

"Nay, more, let this strange thing walk, stand, or sit ...

"No blazing star draws more eyes after it."

"Blazing stars" are comets or meteors, both of which are ill omens.

"A monster," Sir Davy Dapper said. "It is some monster."

"She's a varlet," Sir Alexander said.

"Now is my cue to bristle," Sebastian said to himself.

"A naughty pack," Sir Alexander said.

The word "naughty" meant "evil" in a strong sense.

"Pack" meant "baggage."

"That is false," Sebastian said to his father.

"Huh, boy?" Sir Alexander said.

"What you said is false," Sebastian said.

"What's false?" Sir Alexander said. "I say she's naught."

"Naught" meant "wicked and evil."

Sebastian said:

"I say that any tongue except yours that dares to speak so sticks in the throat of a rank villain."

Telling a man that he lied in his throat was a major insult that could lead to a duel to the death.

Sebastian continued:

"Setting yourself aside —"

"So, sir, what then?" Sir Alexander asked.

Sebastian concluded, "— anyone else here had lied."

He was unwilling to directly accuse his father of lying.

Sebastian then said to himself, "I think I shall fit you!"

"Fit you" can mean "have something ready for you." The "something" would be a requital for bad treatment and bad words. It can also mean "act in such a way that I conform to what you believe about me." It can also mean "act in such a way that will give you a fit."

"Lie?" Sir Alexander said.

"Yes," Sebastian said.

"Does Sir Alexander's story concern Sebastian?" Sir Davy Dapper asked.

Sir Alexander said to himself:

"Ah, sirrah boy! Is your blood heated? Does your blood boil? Are you stung? I'll pierce you deeper yet."

He then said out loud:

"Oh, my dear friends, I am that wretched father, and this Sebastian is that son who sees his ruin yet headlong on he does run!"

"Will you love such a poison?" Sir Adam asked Sebastian.

Sir Davy Dapper said, "Bah! Bah!"

"You are all mad!" Sebastian said. "You are all insane!"

Sir Alexander said to Sebastian:

"Thou are sick at heart, yet thou don't feel it. Of all these gentlemen present, what gentleman but thou, knowing that his disease is deadly and mortal, would shun the cure?"

Sir Alexander then said:

"Oh, Master Greenwit, would you to such an idol bow?"

The idol was the woman whom Sir Alexander thought his son loved: Moll Cutpurse.

"Not I, sir," Greenwit said.

Sir Alexander said:

"Here's Master Laxton."

He then asked:

"Has Master Laxton desire for a woman as thou — Sebastian — have?"

"No, not I, sir," Laxton said.

"Sir, I know it," Sir Alexander said.

A person with the name "Lacks Stone (Testicle)" seems unlikely to desire any woman.

"Their good parts are so rare, their bad so common, that I will have naught to do with any woman," Laxton said.

The word "naught" can mean 1) nothing, or 2) evil, or 3) naughty things.

"It is well done, Master Laxton," Sir Davy Dapper said.

Sir Alexander said to Sebastian, "Oh, thou cruel boy, thou would with lust destroy an old man's life. Because thou see I'm halfway in my grave, thou shovel dust upon me. I wish that thou might have thy wish, most wicked, most unnatural!"

"Why, sir, it is thought that Sir Guy Fitzallard's daughter shall wed your son: Sebastian," Sir Davy Dapper said.

"Sir Davy Dapper, I have upon my knees wooed this fond and foolish boy to take that virtuous maiden," Sir Alexander lied.

Sebastian said:

"Listen, you, let me have a word with you, sir.

"You on your knees have cursed that virtuous maiden and have cursed me for loving her, yet do you now thus baffle — hoodwink and disgrace — me to my face? Don't wear out your knees in such entreaties; give me Fitzallard's daughter."

Sebastian wanted to marry Sir Guy Fitzallard's daughter: Mary, but his father was keeping him from marrying her.

"I'll give thee rats-bane rather!" Sir Alexander said.

"Rats-bane" is rat poison.

Sir Alexander did not want his son to marry either Moll Cutpurse or Mary Fitzallard.

"Well, then you know what dish I mean to feed upon," Sebastian said.

If he couldn't have Mary Fitzallard, then he would have Moll Cutpurse. Or pretend to.

"Hark, gentlemen, he swears to have this cutpurse drab to spite my gall," Sir Alexander said.

A "drab" is a "whore." Sir Alexander was talking about Moll Cutpurse.

A gentleman said, "Master Sebastian!"

Sebastian said, "I am deaf to you all. I'm so bewitched, so bound to my desires, that tears, prayers, threats, nothing can quench those fires that burn within me."

He exited.

Sir Alexander said to himself, "Her blood shall quench that fire then."

He then said out loud:

"Don't lose him! Oh, dissuade him, gentlemen!"

He meant: Don't give up on him! Follow him! Convince him not to marry the wrong woman.

"He shall be weaned from his doting for her, I promise you," Sir Davy Dapper said.

"Before his eyes, lay down his shame, my grief, his miseries," Sir Alexander said.

"No more, no more, away!" the gentlemen said.

Everyone except Sir Alexander exited.

Alone, he said to himself:

"I wash a negro, losing both my pains and my expense, but take thy flight, Sebastian.

"I'll be most near thee when I'm least in sight. I will be aware of what you do even when you can't see me.

"Wild buck, I'll hunt thee breathless; thou shall run on, but I will turn thee and make thou face me when I'm not thought upon."

Washing a black person will not turn black skin white. Sir Alexander was saying his attempt to have his son marry a "suitable" woman was fruitless — so far.

Ralph Trapdoor entered the scene. He was holding a letter.

Sir Alexander said:

"Now, sirrah, who are you? Stop your ape's tricks and speak!"

Ralph Trapdoor had been excessively bowing to him.

"I have a letter from my captain to your worship," Trapdoor said.

Trapdoor had been a soldier; now he was discharged. At least, he claimed to have been a soldier.

"Oh. Oh, now I remember," Sir Alexander said. "It is to recommend thee into my service."

"To be a shifter under your worship's nose of a clean trencher when there's a good bit upon it," Trapdoor said.

As his employee, Trapdoor would eat at Sir Alexander's expense. He would shift — remove — the plates and eat the leftovers.

A "shifter" is also a con man, a cheater. Trapdoor was so good a cheater that he could steal a plate while there was lots of uneaten food on it.

In a more innocent con, comedian Eddie Cantor (1892-1964) worked as a waiter when he was young. He became expert at whisking away diners' half-eaten desserts so he could finish eating them.

Sir Alexander said:

"That is true, honest fellow."

He then said to himself:

"Hmm, huh, let me see.

"This knave shall be the axe to hew that down at which I stumble; he has a face that promises much of a villain. I will grind and sharpen his wit, and if the edge proves to be fine, I will make use of it."

He then said out loud:

"Come here, sirrah. Can thou be secret, huh?"

"I can be as secret as two crafty attorneys plotting the undoing of their clients," Trapdoor said.

"Did thou ever, as thou have walked about this town, hear of a wench called Moll: mad, merry Moll?" Sir Alexander asked.

"Moll Cutpurse, sir?" Trapdoor asked.

"The same," Sir Alexander said. "Do thou know her then?"

Trapdoor said:

"As well as I know that it will rain on the next Simon and Jude's day."

Simon and Jude's day was October 28, the day before the Lord Mayor's outdoor pageant. Bad weather on October 28 could postpone the festivities scheduled for the following day.

Trapdoor continued:

"I will sift all the taverns in the city and drink half-pots with all the watermen at the Bankside, but if you want me to, sir, I'll find her out."

The watermen ferried passengers across the Thames River.

Sir Alexander said:

"That task is easy; do it then.

"Hold thy hand up. What's this? Is it burnt?"

Some convicted felons were branded on their thumb.

"No, sir, no, it is a little singed with making fireworks," Trapdoor said.

Hmm. Maybe.

Sir Alexander gave him money and said to him, "There's money, spend it; that being spent, fetch more."

"Oh, sir, I wish that all the poor soldiers in England had such a leader!" Trapdoor said. "For fetching, no water spaniel is like me."

The English water spaniel, which is now extinct, was used in hunting waterfowl. It had the ability to dive underwater like a duck. There were, however, several varieties of water spaniel.

Sir Alexander said, "This wench we speak of strays so from her kind that Nature repents she made her. It is a mermaid that has tolled — enticed — my son to shipwreck."

At this time, mermaids were often conflated with sirens. Sirens would sing a song that lured sailors to their death.

Ulysses was able to hear the song of the sirens by having his men tie him to a mast so that he would not jump overboard and swim to the sirens, who would have feasted on him.

Sir Alexander was likening the song of the sirens to the tolling of a funeral bell.

A slang meaning of "mermaid" was "whore."

"I'll cut her comb for you," Trapdoor said.

He meant that he would humble and emasculate her: He would take away her masculine traits. When cocks — roosters — were castrated, their combs were also often cut.

Sir Alexander said, "I'll count out gold coins for thee then; hunt her forth. Cast out a line hung full of silver hooks to catch her to thy company. Deep spendings may draw a woman who is very chaste to a man's bosom."

Trapdoor said, "The jingling of golden bells and a good fool with a hobbyhorse will draw all the whores in the town to dance in a morris."

The "jingling" can be made by gold coins as well as by the bells worn by the morris dancer.

A hobbyhorse can be a horse costume worn by a dancer in a morris dance.

It can also be a child's toy: a stick with a horse's head at one end. Figuratively, it would be an erect penis.

A morris dance was usually a country dance, but here it may mean wild dancing.

"Or rather — for that's best because they say sometimes she goes in breeches — follow her as her serving-man," Sir Alexander said.

"And when her breeches are off, she shall follow — obey — me," Trapdoor said.

"Beat all thy brains to serve her," Sir Alexander said.

One kind of "service" is sexual service.

"By God's wounds, sir, as country wenches beat cream until butter comes," Trapdoor said.

This kind of butter can be "cum," aka "man-butter." The "cream" can be vaginal lubrication.

"Play thou the subtle spider, weave fine nets to ensnare her very life," Sir Alexander said.

"Her life?" Trapdoor asked.

Did Sir Alexander want Moll Cutpurse dead?

Sir Alexander said, "Yes, suck her heart-blood — her life-blood — if thou can. Twist thou just cords to catch her, I'll find law to hang her up."

He could get her executed by hanging.

"Spoke like a worshipful bencher — like a magistrate or judge," Trapdoor said.

"Trace — follow — all her steps," Sir Alexander said. "At this she-fox's den, watch what lambs enter: let me play the shepherd to save their throats from bleeding and cut hers."

"This is the goll — the hand — that shall do it," Trapdoor said.

Sir Alexander said:

"Be firm and gain me for always thine own. This done, I employ thee."

If Trapdoor succeeded in taming Moll Cutpurse and stopping Sebastian from marrying her, then Sir Alexander would become Trapdoor's friend and patron.

Sir Alexander then asked:

"What is thy name?"

Trapdoor answered, "My name, sir, is Ralph Trapdoor: honest Ralph."

Sir Alexander said, "Trapdoor, be like thy name, a dangerous step for her to venture on, but unto me —"

Trapdoor finished Sir Alexander's sentence: "— I will be as fast as your sole to your boot or shoe, sir."

"Hence then, be as little seen here as thou can," Sir Alexander said. "I'll always be at thine elbow."

Trapdoor said:

"The trapdoor's set.

"Moll, if you budge, you are gone; this shall crown me.

"A roaring boy the Roaring Girl puts down."

The Roaring Girl will put down his erect penis.

"God-a-mercy," Sir Alexander said. "Lose no time."

"God-a-mercy" means "God have mercy."
They exited.

CHAPTER 2

— 2.1 —

Three shops stood in a row. The first was an apothecary's shop, the next was a feather shop, and the third was a sempster's shop. Sempsters sew and mend clothing.

Mistress Gallipot was in the apothecary's shop, Mistress Tiltyard was in the feather shop, and Master Openwork and his wife were in the sempster's shop. "Mistress" here means "Mrs."

Laxton, Goshawk, and Greenwit entered the scene.

"Gentlemen, what is it you lack?" Mistress Openwork said to them as she tried to get their business. "What is it you buy? See fine collars and ruffs, fine lawns, fine cambrics! What is it you lack, gentlemen? What is it you buy?"

"What is it you lack?" was the standard cry of a shopkeeper.

Lawns and cambrics were types of linen.

"Yonder is the shop," Laxton said.

"Is that she?" Goshawk asked.

He meant Mistress Gallipot.

"Peace," Laxton said. "Be quiet."

"That is she who minces tobacco," Greenwit said.

Tobacco was sold at apothecary shops.

Laxton said, "Aye, she's a gentlewoman born, I can tell you, although it is her hard fortune now to shred Indian pot-herbs."

He was talking about Mistress Gallipot, who prepared tobacco and medicines for sale.

"Pot-herbs" are usually herbs boiled in a pot. North American tobacco was seen as a nourishing herb, and tobacco smoke was reputed to produce many health benefits.

"Oh, sir, it is many a good woman's fortune, when her husband turns bankrupt, to begin with pipes and set up again," Goshawk said.

Pipes can be 1) tobacco pipes, or 2) penises.

Laxton said, "And indeed the raising of the woman is the lifting up of the man's head at all times. If one flourishes, the other will bud as fast, I promise you."

The "head" can be the end of a penis. The raising of a woman's skirt can result in the lifting up of a penis. If the penis flourishes, the woman will "bud": become pregnant.

Laxton, however, was saying that when a woman does well financially, it also economically raises up her husband.

"Come, thou are familiarly acquainted there," Goshawk said. "I grope that."

The word "grope" can mean "grasp" and "understand" in addition to its sexual meaning.

Laxton said, "If you grope no better in the dark, you may perhaps lie in the ditch when you are drunk."

"In the ditch" can mean "in the body cavity." If the man is a bad groper and is drunk, and his aim is impaired, then the body cavity may not be a vagina but a hole that is located close to it.

"Bah, thou are a mystical lecher: a secret seducer," Goshawk said.

"I will not deny but my credit may take up — buy — an ounce of pure smoke," Laxton said.

Goshawk said:

"Your credit may take up an ell of pure smock! Away! Go!"

An ell is 45 inches.

A smock is a woman's undergarment. Its length can be 45 inches.

"Take up" can mean "lift."

Goshawk said to himself:

"He is the closest striker: the most secretive fornicator. By God's life, I think he commits venery forty feet underground; no man is aware of it."

Is Laxton impotent? No one is aware of any affairs of his. Or is he very secretive and does not tell tales?

Goshawk continued saying to himself:

"I like a palpable smockster — a bawd — to go to work so openly with the tricks of art that I'm as clearly seen as a naked boy in a vial."

"Naked boys" are the flowers of meadow saffron. They can be displayed in a clear glass vase.

A naked boy in a vial can be a male fetus in a specimen jar. The fetus ought to be unseen in a womb, and Goshawk's affairs ought to be as unseen as his naked penis in a vagina.

Goshawk liked to know where he and others stood. (Pun intended.) If bawds were open about their work, it was easier for Goshawk to get what he wanted. If women made it clear that they wanted to be seduced, seduction would be much easier.

Goshawk continued saying to himself:

"And were it not for a gift of treachery that I have in me to betray my friend Openwork when he puts most trust in me — by the mass, yonder he is, too — and by his injury to make good my access to her, I should appear as defective in courting as a farmer's son the first day of his feather — newly fledged — who does nothing at court but woo the wall hangings and glass windows — that is, be a wallflower — for a month together, and woo some broken — deflowered — waiting-woman forever after."

Goshawk wanted to seduce Mistress Openwork.

"The first day of his feather" can be "his day of introduction to court."

People at court often wore dyed feathers.

The farmer's son may have practiced bowing and being courtly in front of wall hangings and windows. The glass windows may have reflected an image of the farmer's son's bowing that he could study.

Goshawk continued saying to himself:

"I find those imperfections in my venery that were it not for flattery and falsehood, I should lack discourse and impudence, and he who lacks impudence among women is worthy to be kicked out at beds' feet.

"Openwork shall not see me yet."

"Truly, this tobacco is finely shred," Greenwit said.

"Oh, women are the best mincers," Laxton said.

In other words: Women are the best at chopping things finely, and they are the best at mincing words. They are best at prevaricating and at metaphorically cutting a person up into small pieces. They are also best at walking daintily.

Mistress Gallipot said, "It — 'the best mincers' — would have been a good phrase for a cook's wife, sir."

Laxton said, "But it will serve generally, like the front of a new almanac, as thus: 'Calculated for the meridian of cooks' wives, but generally for all Englishwomen.'"

The front of a new almanac would attempt to make it appeal to as many people as possible. The almanac might have been written especially for the people of London, but the front of the new almanac would say that it could serve for everybody in England. This would increase sales.

Here is a dedication that has a similar purpose:

"TO John Smith WHOM I HAVE KNOWN IN DIVERS AND SUNDRY PLACES ABOUT THE WORLD, AND WHOSE MANY AND MANIFOLD VIRTUES DID ALWAYS COMMAND MY ESTEEM, I Dedicate this Book.

"It is said that the man to whom a volume is dedicated, always buys a copy. If this prove true in the present instance, a princely affluence is about to burst upon

"*THE AUTHOR.*"

This is Mark Twain's dedication for his book *The Celebrated Jumping Frog of Calaveras County and Other Sketches.*

A meridian helps to identify a geographical location.

According to the *Oxford English Dictionary*, "meridian" can mean, "The point or period of highest development or perfection, after which decline sets in; culmination, full splendour."

And the almanac could be written for the most perfect cooks' wives.

"You shall have the pipe, sir," Mistress Gallipot said. "I have filled it for you."

She lit the tobacco in the pipe.

Laxton said, "The pipe's in a good hand, and I wish mine always so."

A "pipe" can be a penis.

"But not to be used in that fashion," Greenwit said.

Mistress Gallipot was putting the pipe to the fire: She was lighting the tobacco. If Laxton's "pipe" — his penis — was to be figuratively set on fire, it would be infected with venereal disease.

Laxton said:

"Oh, pardon me, sir, I understand no French."

Syphilis was called the "French disease." "French" was also slang for "improper language."

Greenwit took off his hat and bowed.

Laxton said to Greenwit:

"Please be covered: Put on your hat."

He then handed Goshawk a pipe and said:

"Jack, have a pipe of rich smoke."

"Jack" is a word similar to "pal." It is a word used in familiar address.

"Rich smoke?" Goshawk said. "That's sixpence a pipe, isn't it?"

"A pipe for me, sweet lady," Greenwit said.

Mistress Gallipot whispered to Laxton, "Don't forget. Respect my reputation. Seem to be a stranger to me. Pretend you don't know me. Art and wit make a fool of suspicion; please be wary."

Laxton whispered back:

"Of course! I promise you that I will!"

He then said out loud to his friends:

"Come, how is it, gallants?"

"Pure and excellent," Greenwit said.

Laxton said:

"I thought it was good because you were grown so silent. You are like those who don't like to talk at meals, although they make a worse noise in the nose than a common fiddler's apprentice and discourse a whole supper with snuffling."

Greenwit was silent because he so enjoyed the tobacco.

Laxton then whispered to Mistress Gallipot:

"I must speak a word with you right away."

Mistress Gallipot whispered back, "Make your way wisely then."

Goshawk said to Greenwit about the quality of the tobacco, "Oh, what else, sir? Laxton is perfection itself, full of manners, but not an acre of ground belonging to him."

Laxton may have manners, but he has no manors.

Greenwit replied, "Aye, and Laxton is full of form: He never has a good stool in his chamber."

The word "form" can mean 1) propriety, and 2) bench.

The word "chamber" can mean 1) room, or 2) chamber pot.

The word "stool" can mean 1) a piece of furniture, or 2) something you can find in a chamber pot.

A bench is a less classy piece of furniture than a chair or a stool.

Laxton may lack stools to sit on and may frequently empty his chamber pot.

Goshawk said, "But Laxton is above all religious: He preys — and prays — daily upon elder brothers."

Laxton prays with old Puritans, and he preys on old men. If Laxton has older brothers, he could be often asking them for money since it was usually the oldest brother who inherited the bulk of an estate.

"And Laxton is valiant above measure," Greenwit said. "He has run three streets from a sergeant.

Sergeants had the power to arrest delinquent debtors.

Laxton coughed. As he coughed, he blew smoke in the faces of Greenwit and Goshawk, who then also coughed.

Greenwit and Goshawk moved away from Laxton.

"What's the matter now, sir?" Mistress Gallipot asked Laxton quietly.

"I protest that I'm in extreme need of money," Laxton said. "If you can supply me now with any means, you do me the greatest pleasure, next to the bounty of your love, as ever poor gentleman tasted."

"What's the sum that would pleasure you, sir?" Mistress Gallipot said. "Although you deserve nothing less at my hands."

What is the "nothing less"? Pleasure? A sum of money?

The pleasure can be sexual, and she can provide it with her hands. Perhaps Laxton deserved nothing less than sexual pleasure and/or money at her hands.

According to the *Oxford English Dictionary*, an obsolete meaning of "nothing less" is "*Anything rather than the thing in question. Often used to express denial: far from it.*"

Laxton, therefore, perhaps deserved anything other than sexual pleasure and/or money: The last thing he deserved from her was sexual pleasure and/or money.

Laxton replied:

"Why, it is but for want of opportunity, thou know."

Mistress Gallipot wanted to have an affair with Laxton, but Laxton would not sleep with her, always saying that he would like to, but that they lacked the opportunity to be intimate.

Laxton said to himself:

"I put her off with opportunity always. By this light, I hate her except for her being the means to keep me in fashion with gallants, for what I take from her I spend upon other wenches. I bear her in hand always; she has wit enough to rob her husband, and I have ways enough to consume the money."

He approached Goshawk from behind and slapped him on the back and asked:

"Why, how are thou now?"

He either hit him too hard or startled him, and Goshawk cried out.

Laxton asked him:

"What! Do you have the chin-cough?"

The "chin-cough" is the whooping cough.

"Thou have the cowardliest trick to come before a man's face and strangle him before he is aware you are there!" Goshawk complained. "I could find in my heart to make a quarrel in earnest."

Laxton said:

"Pox! If thou do — thou know I never am accustomed to fight with my friends — thou'll just lose thy labor in it."

Jack Dapper and his serving-man Gull entered the scene.

Laxton said:

"Jack Dapper!"

Greenwit said, "Monsieur Dapper, I dive down to your ankles."

He made a low bow.

"May God save ye gentlemen, all three in a peculiar — single — salute," Jack Dapper said.

He bowed to Greenwit, Goshawk, and Laxton.

Goshawk whispered to Laxton, "He would be ill as a lawyer: He dispatches three at once."

Jack Dapper had bowed one time; he had not bowed one time each to Laxton, Goshawk, and Greenwit.

If he were a lawyer, it would be financially better for him to deal with clients and solve their legal problems separately rather than in a group.

Laxton whispered back:

"So, well said."

Mistress Gallipot gave him a package of money.

Pretending that the package of money was a package of tobacco, Laxton said to Mistress Gallipot:

"But is this of the same tobacco, Mistress Gallipot?"

He was pretending that she had given him tobacco so the others wouldn't know.

"The same you had at first, sir," Mistress Gallipot said.

"I wish it no better," Laxton said. "This will serve to drink at my chamber."

In this society, the word "drink" in this context meant "smoke."

"Shall we taste a pipe of it?" Goshawk asked.

"Not of this, by my truth, gentlemen," Laxton said. "I have sworn before you."

"What!" Goshawk said. "Not Jack Dapper?"

In other words: You aren't going to treat Jack Dapper with your tobacco?

Laxton said:

"Pardon me, sweet Jack, I'm sorry I made such a rash oath, but foolish oaths must stand.

"Where are thou going, Jack?"

"Indeed, to buy one feather," Jack Dapper said.

Laxton said to himself, "One feather? The fool's peculiar — singular — still."

Jack Dapper then said to his man-servant, "Gull."

"Master," Gull replied.

"Here's three halfpence for your ordinary, boy," Jack Dapper said. "Meet me an hour hence in St. Paul's."

An ordinary is an eating-place. Jack Dapper had given his servant, Gull, money for food.

Gull said to himself:

"What! Three single halfpence! By God's life, this will scarcely serve a man in sauce: a halfpence of mustard, a halfpence of oil, and a halfpence of vinegar. What's left then to pay for the pickled herring?

"This shows like small beer — weak beer — in the morning after a great surfeit of wine overnight."

In other words: Small beer is a hair of the dog that bit you. Food that you can buy for one and a half penny for breakfast is like a bite of the feast you ate the night before.

Gull continued saying to himself:

"Jack could spend his three pounds last night in a supper among girls and splendid bawdy-house boys; I thought his pockets cackled not for nothing. These are the eggs of three pounds; I'll go eat them up right away."

A bawdy-house is a brothel.

The "cackling" was the clinking that Jack Dapper's coins had made in his pocket.

The three halfpence were "eggs": the remains of the three pounds Jack Dapper had spent the previous night. Birds cackle when they lay eggs, and Jack Dapper's three one-pound coins had cackled when they lay half-pence.

Gull exited.

Jack Dapper drifted slowly over to the feather shop.

Counting his money, Laxton said to himself:

"Eight, nine, ten angels."

Angels are gold coins.

He then said, still to himself.

"A good wench, indeed, and one who loves darkness well: She puts out a candle (like a prostitute) with the best tricks of any drugster's wife in England.

"But what makes her mad is that I always find excuses and complain that we have no opportunity to have sex and take no notice of her attempts at seduction.

"The other night she would necessarily lead me into a room with a candle in her hand to show me a naked picture, where we no sooner entered but the candle was sent on an errand."

Mistress Gallipot's showing Laxton a picture of a naked person was intended to make him lustful. She had sent the candle on an errand: She had blown it out.

Laxton continued saying to himself:

"Now I not intending to understand her, but, like a puny — a novice — at the inns of venery, called for another light innocently."

"Understand" includes a pun on "stand," which can mean "erection."

Laxton continued saying to himself:

"Thus I reward all her cunning with simple mistaking. I know she cheats her husband to financially keep me, and I'll keep her honest as long as I can to make the poor man some part of amends: I have an honest and virtuous mind for a whoremaster — for a lecher!"

Laxton then said out loud:

"What do you think among you?

"What! A fresh pipe? Draw in a third man."

Goshawk and Greenwit were sharing a bowl of tobacco, and Laxton was asking to be a third who would share the bowl.

"No, you're a hoarder; you engross — monopolize — by the ounces," Goshawk said.

Laxton was not sharing his "tobacco" (actually, he had received only money from Mistress Gallipot), and so Goshawk would not share this tobacco.

Meanwhile, at the feather shop, Jack Dapper said about a feather, "Bah, I don't like it."

Mistress Tiltyard said, "What feather is it you would have, sir? These feathers are the most worn and are the most in fashion among the beaver gallants, the stone riders, the private stage's audience, the twelvepenny-stool gentlemen. I can inform you it is the general fashion for a feather."

"Beaver gallants" are fashionable men who wear hats made of beaver fur.

"Stone riders" are men who ride stallions. Since "stone" can mean "testicle," "stone riders" may also mean "homosexuals."

Tickets for a play performance on a private stage were expensive.

Twelve pennies for the use of a stool were twice the normal number.

Jack Dapper said:

"And therefore I mislike it; tell me of general! May a continual Simon and Jude's rain now beat down all your feathers as flat as pancakes.

"Show me a spangled feather."

"Spangled" meant 1) "speckled," or 2) "covered with spangles."

Mistress Tiltyard said, "Oh, to go a-feasting with? You'd have it for a henchboy: a page. You shall have it."

According to the *Oxford English Dictionary*, a rare meaning of "feast" is "To enjoy oneself, to make merry."

A henchboy is a young male servant.

Mistress Tiltyard was subtly criticizing Jack Dapper's taste in feathers. He had rejected the fashionable feather; now she was saying that he wanted a feather that was suitable for a servant — or perhaps was suitable for enjoying oneself (homosexually) with a boy-servant.

Meanwhile, at the sempster's shop, Openwork said, "By the mass, I had quite forgotten his honor's footman was here last night, wife. Have you finished with my lord's shirt?"

Mistress Openwork said:

"What's that to you, sir?

"I was this morning at his honor's lodging before such a snail as you crept out of your shell."

Snails have tentacles that look like horns, and so do cuckolds. People in this society joked that men with unfaithful wives had invisible horns on their head.

"Oh, it was well done, good wife!" Openwork said.

"I hold it better, sir, than if you had done it yourself," Mistress Openwork said.

If she had cuckolded her husband that morning, she was saying now that the nobleman was better in bed than her husband was.

"So say I," Openwork said. "But is the countess' smock almost done, mouse?"

"Mouse" was a term of endearment, like "sweetheart" or "dear."

"Here, yes, the cambric, sir, but it lacks the finishing touches, I am afraid," Mistress Openwork said.

"I'll resolve you of that presently," Openwork said. "I'll take care of that right away."

He took the countess' smock and retired with it.

Mistress Openwork said:

"Heyday! Oh, audacious groom, do you dare to presume to work on noblewomen's linen?"

A smock was regarded as intimate apparel.

Mistress Openwork continued:

"Keep your yard to measure shepherd's holland!"

A "yard" is 1) a yardstick, or 2) a penis.

"Holland" was a type of cloth used to make shepherds' clothing.

Mistress Openwork continued:

"I must confine — limit and restrict — you, I see that."

Meanwhile, at the tobacco shop, Goshawk asked Laxton, "What do you say about this gear — about this tobacco?"

Laxton answered, "I dare the arrantest and strictest critic in tobacco to lay one fault upon it."

Moll Cutpurse entered the scene in a frieze jerkin and a black safeguard.

She was wearing a woolen soldier's jacket and an outer petticoat that was used to protect her clothing from dirt and mud when she was riding on horseback. Her attire was partly for males and partly for females.

"By God's life, yonder's Moll!" Goshawk said.

"Moll?" Laxton said. "Which Moll?"

"Honest Moll," Goshawk answered.

Laxton said:

"Please, let's call her."

He called:

"Moll!"

Goshawk and Greenwit called, "Moll, Moll, pist, Moll!"

"How are things now?" Moll Cutpurse asked. "What's the matter?"

"Will you have a pipe of good tobacco, Moll?" Goshawk asked.

"I cannot stay," Moll Cutpurse replied.

"Nay, Moll, bah!" Goshawk said. "Please listen, just one word, indeed."

"Well, what is it?" Moll Cutpurse asked.

"Please come hither, sirrah," Greenwit said.

The word "sirrah" could be used to address both males and females.

Looking at Moll Cutpurse, Laxton said to himself:

"By God's heart, I would give but too much money to be nibbling with that wench! By God's life, she has the spirit of four great parishes, and a voice that will drown all the city; I think a brave captain might beget all his soldiers upon her and never be obliged to use a company of Mile End milksops if he could come on and come off quick enough."

Mile End was a place where London citizen militia trained in military drills. The citizen militia was often criticized.

"Come on and come off" means 1) advance and retreat, and 2) have sex with a woman.

Laxton continued saying to himself:

"Such a Moll would be a marrow-bone before an Italian; he would cry *bona roba* until his ribs were nothing but bone."

A *bona roba* is a prostitute. Literally, it is "good stuff."

"Marrow-bone," like many other foods and drinks, was believed to be an aphrodisiac.

A stereotype of Italians was that they were full of lust.

Laxton continued saying to himself:

"I'll lay hard siege to her; money is that *aqua fortis* that eats into many a maidenhead. Where the walls are flesh and blood, I'll always pierce through with a golden auger."

Aqua fortis is nitric acid.

His "auger" was his penis.

Goshawk said, "Now tell us thy judgment, Moll. Isn't it good?"

Moll Cutpurse said:

"Yes, indeed, it is very good tobacco. For how much do you sell an ounce? Farewell. May God be with you, Mistress Gallipot."

"Why, Moll! Moll!" Goshawk said.

He wanted her to stay.

"I cannot stay now, indeed," Moll Cutpurse said. "I am going to buy a shag ruff; the shop will be shut up presently."

"Shag" is a kind of cloth with velvet nap on one side.

She left to go to the sempster's shop. To get there, she had to pass the feather shop.

"She is the maddest, fantasticalest girl," Goshawk said. "I never knew so much flesh and so much nimbleness put together."

Laxton said:

"She slips from one company to another, like a fat eel between a Dutchman's fingers."

The Dutch were supposed to be fond of butter and eels.

Laxton then said to himself:

"I'll watch my time for her."

He wanted to sleep with her.

Mistress Gallipot said, "Some will not hesitate to say she's a man, and some will not hesitate to say she's both man and woman."

Some people thought that Moll Cutpurse was a hermaphrodite.

"That would be excellent," Laxton said. "She might first cuckold the husband and then make him do as much for the wife."

In other words: Moll Cutpurse might have sex first with the wife and then with the husband.

Meanwhile, at the feather shop, Moll said, "May God save you. How is Mistress Tiltyard doing?"

"Moll," Jack Dapper said.

"Jack Dapper," Moll Cutpurse said.

"How are you doing, Moll?" Jack Dapper asked.

"I'll tell thee by and by," Moll Cutpurse said. "I am going to the next shop."

"Thou shall find me here for this next hour inquiring about a feather," Jack Dapper said.

Moll Cutpurse replied:

"If a feather holds you in play a whole hour, a goose will last you all the days of your life."

A "feather" can be "something resembling a feather. If the "feather" is a penis, then the "goose," in the slang of the time, is a woman or a prostitute.

She went to the sempster shop and said:

"Let me see a good shag ruff."

Openwork said, "Mistress Mary, that shall thou, indeed, and the best in the shop."

But Mistress Openwork said:

"How are things now! Greetings? Love-terms with a pox between you! Have I found out one of your haunts?"

Mistress Openwork suspected that her husband was sleeping with Moll Cutpurse.

Mistress Openwork continued:

"I send you for hollands, and you're in the low countries with a mischief."

"Holland" is 1) linen, and 2) a low country. (Part of the Netherlands is below sea level.)

"The low countries" are also those sexual parts under the bellybutton. They are the nether "lands."

Mistress Openwork continued:

"I'm served with good ware by the shift, which makes it lie dead so long upon my hands."

"Served" can mean "sexual service."

"Ware" can refer to sexual parts.

A "shift" is 1) a lady's chemise, and/or 2) a trick.

In other words: She has good sexual parts next to her undergarment, but since her husband is not raising her shift and making use of her sexual parts, she has to make do with her hands although she would prefer intercourse to masturbation.

"To die" can mean "to have an orgasm."

And/or, possibly: Openwork sometimes has to make shift with her, his wife, when he can't find someone else, but he can't get an erection when he is with her. His affairs use up his sexual energy.

Mistress Openwork continued:

"I would as good shut up shop, for when I open it, I take nothing."

"Take nothing" can mean "earn nothing," or it can mean "get nothing."

"No thing" is "no penis."

In other words: When I open my shop — my legs — for you, I get nothing inside me.

Instead of having sex with Mistress Openwork, her husband may be having sex with other women.

"Nay, once you fall a-ringing your bells — that is, scolding me — the devil cannot stop you," Openwork said. "I'll be out of the belfry as fast as I can, Moll."

Mistress Openwork said to Moll Cutpurse, "Get out of my shop."

"I came here to buy something," Moll Cutpurse said.

"I'll sell you nothing," Mistress Openwork said. "I warn you to stay away from my house and shop."

The shop was in the front of the building, and the living quarters were in the back.

Moll Cutpurse said:

"You goody — goodwife — Openwork, you who prick out a poor living and sew many a bawdy skin-coat — coat made of skins — together —"

A "prick" can be a penis.

A "skin-coat" can be a person's skin. According to Moll Cutpurse, Mistress Openwork sews many skin-coats together — she has sex with many men, and/or she is a bawd.

Moll Cutpurse continued:

"— thou private pandress between shirt and smock — between man and woman — I wish thee for a minute to be a man. Thou should never use more shapes."

A "shape" can be the cut of a garment. But if Mistress Openwork were to assume the shape of a man, Moll Cutpurse would kill her and Mistress Openwork would be unable to assume any other shape.

Moll Cutpurse continued:

"But as thou are a woman, I would pity you if I were to take my revenge. Now my spleen's — my anger's — up, I would not mock it willingly, if I were you.

"Ha! Be thankful."

A fellow with a long rapier by his side entered the scene.

A royal proclamation of 1562 restricted the length of swords. A long sword gave a person an advantage in a fight.

Moll Cutpurse continued:

"Now I forgive thee."

"By the Virgin Mary, hang thee," Mistress Overwork said. "I never asked forgiveness in my life."

Seeing the fellow with the long rapier, Moll Cutpurse said, "You! Goodman swine's-face!"

"What!" the fellow said. "Will you murder me?"

"You remember, slave, how you abused — insulted — me the other night in a tavern?" Moll Cutpurse asked.

"Not I, by this light," the fellow said.

"This light" is the sun.

Moll Cutpurse said:

"No, but by candlelight you did. You have tricks to save your oaths, you have reservations, and I have reserved something for you."

She hit him, and then she said:

"As you like that, call for more; you know the sign again."

The fellow said:

"A pox on it. If I had brought any company along with me to have borne witness of it, it would never have grieved me, but to be struck and nobody nearby, it is my ill fortune still.

"Why, tread upon a worm, they say it will turn tail, but indeed a gentleman should have more manners."

Two expressions were being conflated here:

1) "Even a worm will turn." In other words: Push a normally docile person too far, and he will retaliate.

2) "Turn tail and run." This is a sign of cowardice.

In this society, a gentleman will stick up for himself and not turn tail and run away.

The fellow did not want to fight a woman, but he would have been willing to have her arrested if he had had witnesses.

The fellow with the long rapier exited.

Laxton said, "Gallantly performed, indeed, Moll, and manfully! I love thee forever for it! Base rogue! Had he offered but the least counterblow, by this hand I was prepared for him."

Moll Cutpurse said, "You prepared for him! Why should you be prepared for him? Was he any more than a man?"

"No, nor so much by a yard-and-a-handful London measure," Laxton said.

A "yard" is 1) three feet, 2) a yardstick, or 3) a penis.

A London measure is a yard and a handful: a yard and the width of a hand.

A London measure is little more than the exact measure. London drapers commonly used a London measure.

"Why do you speak this then?" Moll Cutpurse asked. "Do you think I cannot ride a stone horse unless someone leads him by the snaffle — by the bridle-bit?"

Laxton said:

"Yes, and sit him bravely; I know thou can, Moll. It was but an honest mistake through love, and I'll make amends for it any way."

Moll Cutpurse could sit on him — the fellow — in the cowgirl sexual position.

Laxton continued:

"Please, sweet, plump Moll, when shall thou and I go out of town together?"

Moll Cutpurse, who had womanly curves, asked, "Whither? To Tyburn, I ask?"

Tyburn was a place where public executions were held.

Laxton said:

"By the mass, that's out of town indeed; thou hang so many jests upon thy friends still.

"I mean honestly to Brainford, Staines, or Ware."

These were places where lovers met.

"What would we do there?" Moll Cutpurse asked.

"Nothing but be merry and lie together," Laxton said. "I'll hire a coach with four horses."

"Lie together" means "have sex together."

Some sex affairs took place in coaches.

"I thought it would be a beastly journey," Moll Cutpurse said. "You may well leave out one: Three horses will serve if I play the jade myself."

A "jade" can be 1) a poor horse, or 2) a whore.

"Bah, thou are such a kicking wench!" Laxton said. "Please be kind and let's meet."

He wanted an assignation, not a joke.

"It is hard, but we shall meet, sir," Moll Cutpurse said. "It would be a shame if we didn't.

Laxton wanted a part of his body to get hard.

Laxton said:

"Just appoint the place then."

He gave her his money and said:

"There are ten angels in fair gold, Moll; you see I do not trifle with you. Just say thou will meet me, and I'll have a coach ready for thee."

"Why, here's my hand," Moll Cutpurse said. "I'll meet you, sir."

Laxton said to himself:

"Oh, good gold!"

He then asked out loud:

"The place, sweet Moll?"

"It shall be your appointment," Moll Cutpurse said. "You decide."

"Somewhat near Holborn, Moll," Laxton said.

"In Gray's Inn Fields then," Moll Cutpurse said.

"It's a match," Laxton said. "It's a deal."

"I'll meet you there," Moll Cutpurse said.

"The hour?" Laxton asked.

"Three," Moll Cutpurse said.

"That will be time enough to eat at Brainford," Laxton said.

In the meantime, Openwork and Goshawk were talking together at the sempster's shop. In a few moments, Moll Cutpurse and Laxton would walk over to and join them.

Openwork said to Goshawk:

"I am of such a nature, sir, that I cannot endure the house when she scolds. She has a tongue that will be heard further on a still morning than Saint Antling's bell."

St. Antling's is the Puritan church of St. Antholin. In 1599, the loud chapel bell rang at 5 a.m. for early morning religious lectures or services.

Openwork continued:

"She rails upon me for foreign wenching, and she rails that I being a freeman must necessarily keep a whore in the suburbs and seek to impoverish the liberties of the city of London."

London had rules and regulations as well as liberties, and so a whore in the suburbs outside of London could avoid the rules and regulations.

Mistress Openwork wanted her husband to take his sexual liberties at home, with her.

Openwork continued:

"When we fall out and quarrel, I trouble you still to make all whole with my wife."

"No trouble at all," Goshawk said. "It is a pleasure to me to join things together."

Goshawk wanted to seduce Mistress Openwork and join their "things" together.

Openwork said:

"Go thy ways — carry on."

He then said to himself:

"I do this only to test thy honesty, Goshawk."

Meanwhile, at the feather shop, Jack Dapper and Moll Cutpurse were talking.

Wearing some spangled feathers, Jack Dapper asked, "How do thou like this, Moll?"

Moll Cutpurse said:

"Oh, singularly! You're fitted out now with a bunch."

Jack Dapper had come to the shop to buy one feather, but now he was wearing several feathers.

Moll Cutpurse then said to herself:

"He looks for all the world with those spangled feathers like a nobleman's bedpost!"

Noblemen's bedposts were often decorated with feathers.

Moll then said to herself about Mistress Tiltyard:

"I would like to try the purity — the chastity — of your wench; she seems like Kent, unconquered, and I believe as many wiles are in her."

A boast of the citizens of Kent was that Kent had never been conquered by William the Conqueror but had retained its own laws and customs.

"Kent" can sound like "cunt," and "wiles" can sound like the Kentish "wilds": the wild areas and forests of Kent.

Moll continued saying to herself:

"Oh, the gallants of these times are shallow lechers."

"Shallow lechers" do not thrust deeply when having sex.

Moll continued saying to herself:

"They don't put their courtship home — thoroughly — enough to a wench. It is impossible to know what woman is thoroughly honest, because she's never thoroughly tried; I am of that certain belief there are more queans — whores and strumpets — in this town of their own making than of any man's provoking. Where lies the slackness then?"

The slackness lay in penises.

Moll continued saying to herself:

"Many a poor soul would fall away from chastity and have an affair, but there's nobody who will push them.

"Women are courted but never soundly tried …

"As many walk in spurs who never ride."

Some men wear spurs but never ride a horse: The spurs are for show only.

Women may not be soundly courted because men put on a show of being sexually active but never have sex.

Some men don't kiss, but they do tell.

Meanwhile, at the sempster's shop, Mistress Openwork and Goshawk were talking together.

"Oh, abominable!" Mistress Openwork said.

"Nay, more," Goshawk said. "I tell you in private, he keeps a whore in the suburbs."

Openwork had not said that: He had said that his wife believed that he kept a whore in the suburbs.

Goshawk was telling lies about Openwork as part of his plan to seduce Mistress Openwork.

"Oh, spital dealing!" Mistress Openwork said. "I came to him a gentlewoman born. I'll show you my arms when you please, sir."

One kind of arms is a coat of arms.

"Spitals" were hospitals that treated venereal disease.

Goshawk said to himself, "I had rather see your legs and begin that way."

Mistress Openwork said, "It is well known that he took me from a lady's service, where I was well beloved of the steward; I had my Latin tongue and a spice of the French before I came to him, and now he keeps a suburban whore under my nostrils."

Some spices are hot. Burning was associated with syphilis, which was called the French disease.

"There are ways enough to cry quit and get even with him," Goshawk said. "Listen in thine ear."

He whispered to her.

"There's a friend worth a million," Mistress Openwork said.

Moll Cutpurse said to herself: "I'll try one spear against your chastity, Mistress Tiltyard, although it proves too short by the burr."

The "spear" is usually located under a man's bellybutton.

A burr is a broad iron ring; it is located on the handle end of a spear used in jousts.

The "burr" is usually located under a woman's bellybutton.

Moll Cutpurse was going to test Mistress Openwork's chastity, although Moll's clitoris (especially when erect, it was a spear) was shorter than a penis. Moll had a ring (vagina) and she wanted to use a spear (penis) to seduce Mistress Tiltyard. Moll's clitoris (short spear) was by her ring (vagina).

Yes, ladies have their own versions of erections. Clitorate people know this.

Ralph Trapdoor entered the scene.

He said to himself:

"By the mass, here she is! I'm bound by Sir Alexander already to serve her, although it is only a sluttish trick."

"Serve her" may mean 1) serve her as a servant, and/or 2) service her in bed.

Trapdoor then said to Moll Cutpurse:

"Bless my hopeful young mistress with long life and great limbs! Send her the upper hand over all bailiffs and their hungry adherents!"

"How are things now!" Moll Cutpurse said. "Who are thou?"

"I am a poor, ebbing gentleman who would gladly wait for the young flood of your service," Trapdoor said.

A "young flood" is the beginning of a tide up the Thames River. Serving Moll Cutpurse would raise Trapdoor's ebbing — declining — fortunes.

"My service!" Moll Cutpurse said. "What should move you to offer your service to me, sir?"

"The love I bear to your heroic spirit and masculine womanhood," Trapdoor said.

"So, sir, suppose that we should retain you to us, what parts are there in you for a gentlewoman's service?" Moll Cutpurse said.

"Parts" can be sexual parts, and "service" can be sexual service.

Trapdoor said, "My service will be of two kinds, right worshipful Moll Cutpurse. The two kinds are movable and immovable: movable to run on errands, and immovable to stand when you have occasion to use me."

A "stand" is an erection, which can be put to sexual use.

Movable penises are soft and can be bent.

"What strength do you have?" Moll Cutpurse asked.

Good lovers have strong backs.

"Strength, Mistress Moll," Trapdoor said. "I have gone up into a steeple and stopped the great bell as it has been ringing. I have stopped a windmill going."

Trapdoor's words may bring to mind an image of sexual violence. He has stopped a bell from ringing = He has stopped a woman from screaming. He has stopped the arms of a windwill = He has restrained the arms of a woman.

"And never been struck down yourself?" Moll Cutpurse asked.

Has a woman ever avoided his rape?

Trapdoor said, "I have always stood as upright as I do at this moment."

Moll Cutpurse tripped his heels; he fell.

She said to him:

"Come, I pardon you for this; it shall be no disgrace to you. I have struck up the heels of the high German's size before now."

The German was a famous fencer of large size.

She then asked Trapdoor, who was still lying on the ground:

"What! Won't you stand?"

"I am of that nature that where I love, I'll be at my mistress' foot to do her service," Trapdoor said.

A mistress can be 1) a female boss, 2) a woman to whom one is devoted, and/or 3) a woman one sleeps with regularly but is not married to.

"Why, well said," Moll Cutpurse said. "But say that your mistress should receive injury. Have you the spirit of fighting in you? Do you dare to second her? Will you dare to back her up?"

"By God's life, I have kept a bridge myself and have driven seven at a time before me," Trapdoor said.

"Kept" can mean 1) defended, or 2) took care of.

"Aye?" Moll Cutpurse said. "Really?"

Trapdoor nodded "yes" to her and then said to himself:

"But they were all Lincolnshire bullocks, I swear by my truth."

He had driven seven bull calves, not seven enemy soldiers.

Moll Cutpurse said, "Well, meet me in Gray's Inn Fields between three and four this afternoon, and upon better consideration we'll retain you."

Trapdoor said:

"I humbly thank your good mistress-ship."

He then said to himself:

"I'll crack your neck for this kindness."

He would do an evil deed in response to a good deed.

According to the *Oxford English Dictionary*, one definition of "neck" (in anatomy) at this time is "A constricted or narrow part at one end of a saccular organ or structure, esp. the bladder or the uterus."

Trapdoor was talking about having sex with Moll.

His words also applied to Moll's neck being broken in a noose.

Trapdoor exited.

Moll met Laxton.

"Remember," Laxton said. "You will meet me at three."

"If I fail you, hang me," Moll Cutpurse said.

"Good wench, indeed," Laxton said.

He moved away from Moll Cutpurse, and Openwork, who was in a disguise to fool his wife, went over to Moll.

"Who's this?" Moll Cutpurse asked, not recognizing him.

"It is I, Moll," Openwork said.

"Please tend thy shop and prevent bastards," Moll Cutpurse said.

"We'll have a pint of the same wine, indeed, Moll," Openwork said.

"Bastard" was the name of a sweet Spanish wine.

Moll Cutpurse and Openwork exited. A church bell struck, indicating the time.

Goshawk said:

"Listen, the bell rings; come, gentlemen.

"Jack Dapper, where shall we all munch?"

"I am all for going to Parker's ordinary," Jack Dapper said.

An ordinary is an eating-place.

Laxton said:

"He's a good guest to him; he deserves his board. He draws all the gentlemen in a term-time thither."

Jack Dapper may receive, or deserve to receive, free meals because he brings so many diners to the ordinary.

"Term-time" was the period of time the law courts were open.

Laxton continued:

"We'll be your followers, Jack, lead the way."

He then said quietly to Goshawk and Greenwit:

"Look, by my faith, the fool has feathered his nest well."

Jack Dapper had bought one or more feathers.

The gallants — Laxton, Goshawk, Greenwit, and Jack Dapper — exited.

Gallipot, Tiltyard, and some servants entered with water-spaniels and a duck-decoy.

Water spaniels were used in hunting waterfowl.

Tiltyard said:

"Come, shut up your shops."

He then asked:

"Where's Master Openwork?"

"Nay, don't ask me, Master Tiltyard," Mistress Gallipot said.

Tiltyard asked:

"Where's his water-dog?"

He then made sounds to call a dog.

"Come, wenches, come," Gallipot said. "We're going all to Hogsden."

"To Hogsden, husband?" Mistress Gallipot asked.

"Aye, to Hogsden, pigsney," Gallipot replied.

"Pigsney" means "pig's eye." It is a term of endearment.

"I'm not ready, husband," Mistress Gallipot said.

Gallipot said:

"Indeed, that's 'well.'"

He called a dog to him and then spit in the dog's mouth.

People in this society thought that dogs liked that.

Gallipot then said:

"Come, Mistress Openwork, you are taking so long."

"I have no joy in my life, Master Gallipot," Mistress Openwork said.

Gallipot said:

"Bah, let your boy lead his water-spaniel along and we'll show you the bravest sport at Parlous Pond."

Parlous (Perilous) Pond got its name because of the many accidents that happened there. Both duck-hunting and swimming took place there.

Gallipot said:

"Hey, Trug! Hey, Trug! Hey, Trug!"

"Trug" can mean "prostitute."

Here, it may be the name of a dog.

Gallipot then said:

"Here's the best duck in England, except my wife."

A duck is a female; the male is a drake.

"Duck" is a term of endearment. Reports of Gallipot consorting with whores may be greatly exaggerated. His wife's belief that he does this may be incorrect.

He then called the dogs:

"Hey, hey, hey! Fetch, fetch, fetch!

"Come, let's go away.

"Of all the year, this is the most sportful day."

Alone on a street, Sebastian said to himself:

"If a man has a free will, where should its use more perfectly shine than in his will to love?"

Sir Alexander entered the scene and listened to him.

Sebastian continued:

"All creatures have their liberty in that, although otherwise they are kept under servile yoke and fear. The very bondslave has his freedom there.

"Among a world of creatures voiced and silent must my desires wear fetters?"

Seeing Sir Alexander, his father, Sebastian said to himself:

"Are you so near? Then I must break with my heart's truth, meet grief at a back way and grieve privately; well."

He meant that now he would have to put on an act for his father: an act stating his love for Moll Cutpurse. He would have to grieve for Mary Fitzallard later, in private.

Sebastian said out loud:

"Why, suppose the two-leaved tongues of slander or of truth pronounce that Moll Cutpurse is loathsome."

Some doors and gates had two leaves: top and bottom. One leaf (tongue) told truth; one leaf (tongue) told slander. One or the other pronounced Moll Cutpurse to be loathsome. But Sebastian, who knew that his father was eavesdropping on him, said that she appeared beautiful to him.

Sebastian continued:

"If before my loving gaze she appears to be fair, what injury do I have?

"I have the thing I like. In all other things, my own eye guides me, and I find that all these other things prosper and turn out well.

"Life, what should ail it now? Why should something be wrong with my eyesight now? I know that man never truly loves — if he denies it, he lies — who keeps his own eyes shut and marries with his father's eyes."

That man who marries with his father's eyes does not choose his own wife; instead, he allows his father to choose whom he marries.

Sebastian continued:

"I'll keep my own eyes wide open."

Moll Cutpurse and a porter entered the scene. The porter was carrying a viol, which was similar to a modern cello, on his back.

Seeing Moll, Sir Alexander said to himself, "Here's 'brave' willfulness. This is a made match: an arranged meeting. Here she comes; they have met on purpose."

"Must I carry this great fiddle to your chamber, Mistress Mary?" the porter asked.

"Fiddle, goodman hog-rubber?" Moll Cutpurse said. "Some of these porters bear so much for others that they have no time to carry wit for themselves."

Being called a hog-rubber is an insult. It means "yokel."

Moll Cutpurse objected to her viol being called a fiddle. Fiddles had less status than viols.

"To your own chamber, Mistress Mary?" the porter asked.

"Who'll hear an ass — a foolish beast of burden — speak?" Moll Cutpurse said. "Where else, goodman pageant-bearer? They're people of the worst memories."

Porters sometimes carried pageants: portable stages.

She had previously told the porter where to set down the viol. He had already forgotten.

The porter exited.

Sebastian said, "Why, it would be too great a burden, love, to have them carry things in their minds and on their backs together."

"Pardon me, sir," Moll Cutpurse said. "I didn't know you were so near."

Sir Alexander said to himself, "So, so, so."

He was listening intently.

Sebastian said to Moll:

"I would be nearer to thee, and I would be nearer to thee in that fashion that makes the best part — the greatest part — of all creatures honest."

He was referring to marriage with Moll Cutpurse. Of course, he did not want to marry her but instead to marry Mary Fitzallard. He, however, did want his father to think that he wanted to marry Moll.

Sebastian continued:

"I wish it to be no otherwise."

Moll Cutpurse said:

"Sir, I am so poor and unworthy to requite you that you must look for nothing but thanks from me."

She was rejecting his marriage proposal.

Moll Cutpurse continued:

"I have no humor — disposition — to marry. I love to lie on both sides of the bed myself.

"And besides, on the other hand, a wife, you know, ought to be obedient, but I am afraid that I am too headstrong to obey, so therefore I'll never go about it."

In this society, a good wife was an obedient wife.

Moll continued:

"I love you so well, sir, for your good will I'd be loath you should repent your bargain afterward, and therefore we'll never come together in the first place.

"I have the head now of myself and I am man enough for a woman; marriage is but a chopping and changing, where a maiden loses one head and has a worse one in its place."

A maiden who becomes a wife loses her maidenhead and has to obey her husband: the head of the household.

A horse that is given its head is free to move as it wishes without being checked by its rider.

Pleased by Moll's rejection of his son's marriage proposal, Sir Alexander said to himself, "This is the most comfortablest answer from a roaring girl that ever my ears drunk in."

Sebastian said to Moll, "This would be enough now to frighten a fool forever from thee, when it is the music that I love thee for."

Sebastian was saying that he liked a strong woman.

"There's a boy who spoils it all again," Sir Alexander said to himself.

Sebastian seemed to be not giving up on trying to marry Moll.

Moll Cutpurse said to Sebastian, "Believe it, sir, I am not of that disdainful temper, for I could love you faithfully."

She was not so disdainful that it would prevent her from loving him and being faithful to him.

Displeased, Sir Alexander said to himself, "A pox on you for that word! I don't like you now: You are a cunning roarer. I see that already."

He thought that she was playing hard to get but would be happy to marry Sebastian.

Moll Cutpurse said to Sebastian:

"Just sleep upon this once more, sir. You may happen to shift and change your mind tomorrow.

"Don't be too hasty to wrong yourself; never while you live, sir, take a wife running — that is, in haste: many who have done it have run out at heels."

"To be out at heels" means to be impoverished: to have holes in one's stockings and/or shoes.

Moll continued:

"You see, sir, I speak against myself, and if every woman would deal with their suitor so honestly, poor younger brothers would not be so often gulled with old cozening, deceitful widows who turn over all their wealth in trust to some kinsman and make the poor gentleman work hard for a pension."

Younger brothers inherited little or nothing, and so they could attempt to marry for money.

When a man married a rich woman, he gained control of her wealth unless she had made precautions against that. Some women put their wealth in the management of relatives so their husbands would not get it. They would dole out money at times to their husband: They would be their husband's "pension."

Playwright Wilson Mizner (1876-1933) once married a rich society lady, which seemed to be a marriage made in heaven, given Mr. Mizner's great delight in spending money. However, his wife kept a tight grip on her money, giving her husband very little of it. Mr. Mizner once got on his knees and pleaded for an hour with his wife to prove her love for him by signing a blank check, but she would not. While dining at the Waldorf-Astoria, Mr. Mizner was again pleading for money. This so annoyed his wife that she began beating him with the nearest thing she had in her possession — an envelope filled with money. The envelope came open, the money spilled everywhere, and Mr. Mizner and the other diners in the restaurant began scrambling for it. His wife saw him on his knees, picking up money, and she screamed that he could have the money since he was willing to crawl for it. Mr. Mizner said later, "I'd picked up $8,000 before I realized I'd been insulted."

Moll concluded:

"Fare you well, sir."

"Nay, please, one word more," Sebastian said.

Of course, "one word more" meant "more than one word more."

"How I wrong this girl," Sir Alexander said to himself. "She puts him off still!"

Moll said to Sebastian:

"Think upon this in cold blood, sir: You make as much haste as if you were going upon a voyage to fish for sturgeon."

In other words: Don't choose a wife as if you were going to be away from home for long periods of time.

Moll continued:

"Take deliberation, sir; never choose a wife as if you were going to Virginia."

In other words: Don't choose a wife as if women were rare and any woman would do.

In the early 1600s, it was difficult to find a woman who would endure the difficulty of sailing to and living in Virginia.

Moll moved away from him.

Sebastian said, "And so we parted, my too-cursed fate."

He was pretending to be hurt by Moll Cutpurse's rejection of him, knowing that his father would see and hear him.

Sebastian retired a distance away.

Sir Alexander said to himself, "She is just being cunning, giving him longer time in it."

In other words: Moll was like a creditor who gives a debtor more time to repay a debt, thereby allowing the interest to mount.

He thought once more that she was playing hard to get but would be happy to marry Sebastian.

A tailor entered the scene and called for Moll Cutpurse: "Mistress Moll, Mistress Moll. So ho ho so ho!"

This was the cry of a falconer calling a falcon.

Moll called:

"There, boy! There, boy!"

This was the cry of a huntsman calling his dogs.

Moll asked:

"What! Do thou go a-hawking after me with a red cloth on thy finger?"

The red cloth could be 1) a pincushion the tailor has attached to his finger, 2) a cloth to protect a falconer's finger, or 3) a bloodstained bandage.

"I forgot to take your measurements for your new breeches," the tailor said.

Men wore breeches.

Sir Alexander said to himself, "Heyday! Breeches! What! Will my son marry a monster with two trinkets? What age is this? What's the world coming to? If the wife goes about in breeches, the man must wear long petticoats like a fool."

The "two trinkets" may mean "two testicles," or "two sets of genitals," if Moll Cutpurse were a hermaphrodite.

Children, women, fools, and jesters wore long coats or petticoats.

Moll Cutpurse asked, "What fiddling's here? What foolery's this? Wouldn't the old pattern have served your turn?"

"You changed the fashion," the tailor said. "You say you'll have the great Dutch slop, Mistress Mary."

She had ordered wide, baggy breeches.

"Why, sir, I say so still," Moll said.

"Your breeches then will take up a yard more," the tailor said.

"Well, please look that it be put in then," Moll said.

Tailors had a reputation for stealing cloth rather than using all of it to make a customer's clothing, so Moll Cutpurse wanted to make sure that the tailor used the whole extra yard of clothing in making her breeches.

A "yard" can be a penis, and "put in" can mean what you think it can mean.

"It shall stand round and full, I warrant you," the tailor said.

Hmm. "Stand round and full." Say no more.

"Please make them easy enough," Moll Cutpurse said.

She wanted them to be comfortable.

"I know my fault now," the tailor said. "The other was somewhat stiff between the legs; I'll make these open enough, I promise you."

A "fault" can be a vulva.

Penises can be stiff. Vulvas can be open.

Sir Alexander said to himself, "Here's good gear coming! I have brought up my son to marry a Dutch slop and a French doublet, a codpiece-daughter-in-law!"

A "codpiece" was an article of clothing: a pouch for the male genitals.

"Gear" can mean 1) business, and 2) clothing.

The tailor said, "So, I have gone as far as I can go."

He was referring to taking Moll's measurements.

Some young teenaged girls may think that a tailor is "vulgar" or worse when he measures their chest or hips. The inseam is often an important measurement.

"Why then, farewell," Moll Cutpurse said.

"If you go soon to your chamber, Mistress Mary, please send me the measure of your thigh by some honest body," the tailor said.

"Well, sir, I'll send it by a porter presently," Moll Cutpurse said.

Moll exited.

"So you have need to," the tailor said. "Your thigh is a lusty one; both of them would make any porter's back ache in England."

Moll Cutpurse's thighs were lusty: full of healthful vigor.

A strong back is useful when having sex.

The tailor exited.

Sebastian said:

"I have examined the best part of man — reason and judgment — and they tell me that they leave me uncontrolled when I am in love.

"Take a man who is swayed by an unfeeling blood past heat of love: His springtime must needs err. The watch of a person who sets his dial by a rusty clock never goes right."

Men who are too old or too rational cannot be in love well, physically (old men) or emotionally (men who too closely follow reason and judgment). It is best for a young man to ignore reason and judgment and old fathers when in love.

Sir Alexander came forward and said, "So, and which is that rusty clock, sir? You?"

"The clock at Ludgate, sir," Sebastian said. "It never goes true. It never tells the right time."

He did not want to quarrel with his father.

Sir Alexander said:

"But thou go falser. Thy father's cares and worries cannot keep thee right.

"When that insensible work — the clock — obeys the workman's art, it tells off the hour and stops again when time is satisfied."

In other words: When the clock is put in good working order, it chimes the correct time and then stops chiming.

Sir Alexander continued:

"But thou run on, and judgment, thy main wheel, beats by and passes all stops as if the work begun with long pains would break for a minute's ruin."

A "stop" is a mechanism that stops the striker from striking the chime.

According to Sir Alexander, Sebastian could ruin his life in the minute it would take to marry someone whom Sir Alexander did not approve of.

According to Sir Alexander, Sebastian Sebastian does not stop and consider the consequences of his actions.

Sir Alexander continued:

"Much like a suffering man brought up with care at last bequeathed to shame and a short prayer."

The short prayer would be said before an execution.

Sebastian said, "I taste — experience — you bitterer than I can deserve, sir."

Their relationship was bitterer than it should be.

Sir Alexander said:

"Who has bewitched thee, son? What devil or drug has wrought upon the weakness of thy blood and betrayed all her hopes to ruinous folly?

"Oh, wake from drowsy and enchanted shame, wherein thy soul sits with a golden dream, flattered and poisoned!

"I am old, my son. Oh, let me prevail quickly, for I have weightier business of my own than to chide thee.

"I must not go to my grave as a drunkard goes to his bed, whereon he lies only to sleep and never cares to rise.

"Let me settle my affairs in time; go no more near her."

Sebastian said, "Not go near her honestly? Not in the way of marriage?"

"What!" Sir Alexander said. "Do thou say 'marriage'? In what place? The sessions-house — the courthouse? And please tell me who shall give the bride — an indictment?"

"Sir, now you take part with the world to wrong her," Sebastian said.

Sir Alexander said:

"Why, would thou desire to marry to be pointed at? Alas, the number of people who are pointed at because of bad marriages is great; do not overburden it.

"Why, it would be as good for thee to marry a beacon on a hill, which all the people in the country fix their eyes upon, as to marry her whom thy folly dotes on.

"If thou long to have the story of thy infamous fortunes serve for discourse and gossip in ordinaries and taverns, thou are in the right way; or if thou long to confound and ruin thy name and reputation, keep on — thou cannot miss doing it. Or if thou long to strike thy wretched father to untimely coldness and early death — keep the left hand — the perverse and sinister way — still, it will bring thee to it."

In a parable, the young Heracles (Roman name: Hercules) is visited by Virtue and Vice and offered a choice of paths in life. At a fork in the road, the left-hand path leads to an easy life with no glory, while the right-hand path leads to a life of hardship and lots of glory. Similarly, in the *Iliad*, Achilles can choose between a long life and no glory in Greece or an early death and lots of glory at Troy.

Since we know the names of Heracles/Hercules and of Achilles, we know the decision they made.

Sir Alexander continued:

"Yet if no tears wrung from thy father's eyes, nor sighs that fly in sparks from his sorrows, had power to alter what is willful in thee, I think that her very name and reputation should frighten thee away from her and never trouble me."

"Why is the name of Moll so fatal and deadly, sir?" Sebastian asked.

Sir Alexander said, "Many police officers, sir, where suspicion of one Moll is entered in the legal records, forseek — that is, weary themselves in searching thoroughly all London from one end to the other. They weary themselves in seeking for one Moll because there are more whores named 'Moll' than of any other ten names."

Sebastian said:

"What's that to her? Let those blush for themselves. Can any guilt in others condemn her?

"I've vowed to love her. Let all storms oppose me that ever beat against the breast of man. Nothing but death's black tempest shall divide us."

"Oh, folly that can dote on nought — nothing — but shame!" Sir Alexander said.

Sebastian said:

"Suppose the case that a wanton itch runs through one name more than another."

In this society, "case" was slang for "vagina."

In other words: Suppose that whoredom is associated with one name — Moll — than any other.

Sebastian continued:

"Is that name the worse where honesty sits possessed in it? It should rather appear more excellent and deserve more praise when it can raise a brightness through foul mists.

"Why, some in the devil's party are honest gentlemen, and well descended, who keep an open house and are hospitable."

Some of these good people are named "Nick" — after the devil's name. Old Nick is Old **Iniq**uity. "Iniquity" means "immoral behavior."

Sebastian continued:

"And some in the good man's party are arrant knaves."

Some of these arrant knaves are named "Christian" after Christ.

A proverb stated, "God is a good man."

Sebastian continued:

"He hates unworthily who by rote and mindless rules scorns and contemns, for the name neither saves nor yet condemns.

"And as for her honesty, I have made such proof of it — I have tested it — in several forms. So nearly and closely have I watched her ways, I will strictly maintain her honesty against an army, with the exception of you, my father.

"Here's the worst that can be said about her: She has a bold spirit that mingles with Mankind, but nothing else comes near it."

In other words: Mankind — that is, the male sex — comes near Moll's spirit, but near nothing else that belongs to her.

Also in other words: Moll may associate with men, but she does not sleep with them.

Sebastian continued:

"And often through her male apparel she somewhat shames her birth as a female, but she is loose in nothing but in mirth."

In other words: Moll may wear men's clothing, but she does not sleep with men.

Sebastian concluded:

"I wish that all Molls were no worse than she."

Sir Alexander said to himself:

"This way I toil in vain and only give aim to infamy and ruin."

A person who gives aim stands by the target and tells the archer how close an arrow came to the target; for example, the shot may be wide and short of the target. This helps the archer to adjust and perfect his shot. In other words, Sir Alexander's opposition to the marriage seems to do nothing but make his son more determined to marry Moll Cutpurse.

Sir Alexander continued saying to himself:

"He will fall. My blessing cannot stop him.

"All my joys stand at the brink of a devouring flood and will be willfully swallowed, willfully.

"But why let all these tears be lost in vain: I'll pursue her and shame her, and so everything will be crossed and thwarted."

Sir Alexander exited.

Alone, Sebastian said to himself:

"He has gone with some strange purpose, whose effect will hurt me little if he shoots so wide of the mark that he thinks I love so blindly as to really want to marry Moll.

"I just feed his heart to this marriage match to draw on and bring about the other marriage match, wherein my joy sits with a full wish crowned, with only his mood of anger excepted, which must change by policies opposite to what he wants, carried out by indirect courses: Plain dealing in this world takes no effect."

Sebastian was making his father think that he — Sebastian — wanted to marry Moll Cutpurse, but Sebastian was doing that only as part of his plan to get his father's permission for him to marry Mary Fitzallard.

A proverb stated, "Plain dealing is a jewel, but they who use it die beggars."

Sebastian continued saying to himself:

"This mad girl I'll acquaint with my intention and purpose, get her assistance, and make my fortunes and circumstances known to her.

"Between lovers' hearts, she's a fit instrument and has the art to help lovers' hearts to their own — that is, what is rightfully theirs: marriage.

"By her advice, for in that craft she's wise ...

"My love and I may meet, in spite of all spies."

Sebastian exited.

CHAPTER 3

— 3.1 —

Laxton and the coachman stood together in Gray's Inn Fields. The coachman was carrying a whip.

"Coachman," Laxton said.

"Here, sir," the coachman said.

Laxton gave him a coin and said, "There's a tester — a sixpence — more. Please drive thy coach to the hither end of Marybone Park, a fit place for Moll to get in the coach."

"Marybone" calls to mind "marrow bone." The edible marrow in the bone was believed to be an aphrodisiac.

A woman's body can be likened to a park if one is allowed to roam freely there. A woman's body is sometimes a Disneyland for adults.

"Marybone Park, sir?" the coachman asked.

"Aye, it's in our way, thou know," Laxton said.

"It shall be done, sir," the coachman said.

"Coachman," Laxton said.

"Immediately, sir," the coachman said.

"Are we fitted with good frampold — spirited — jades?" Laxton asked.

"The best in Smithfield, I promise you, sir," the coachman said.

Jades are bad horses; Smithfield, which had a market for horses, had a reputation for having jades.

"May we safely take the upper hand of and pass any couched — embroidered with gold — velvet cap or tufftaffety — tufted taffeta — jacket?" Laxton said. "For they keep a vile swaggering in coaches nowadays; the highways are stopped with them."

Newly rich people wore expensive, fancy clothing and frequently used coaches.

The coachman said:

"My life for yours — I bet my life we can. And we can insult them, too, sir, by making it impossible for them to pass us.

"Why, they are the same jades, believe it, sir, that have drawn all your famous whores to the town of Ware."

"Then they know their business," Laxton said. "They need no more instructions."

"They're so used to such journeys, sir, I never use the whip on them, for if they catch just the scent of a wench once, they run like devils," the coachman said.

Carrying his whip, the coachman exited.

Alone, Laxton said to himself:

"He is a fine Cerberus: That rogue will have the head-start of a thousand ones, for while others trot afoot, he'll ride prancing to hell upon a coach-horse."

Cerberus is the three-headed guard dog in the Land of the Dead. Many affairs took place in coaches, and the coachman served as a kind of guard to the fornicators.

Laxton continued saying to himself:

"Wait, it is now about the hour of her appointment, but yet I don't see Moll."

The clock began to strike.

Hearing the clock, Laxton continued saying to himself:

"Hark, what's this? One, two, three — three by the clock at Savoy."

The Savoy was a hospital.

Laxton continued saying to himself:

"This is the hour, and Gray's Inn Fields is the place. She swore she'd meet me. Ha! Yonder are two Inns of Court men with one wench, but that's not she; they walk toward Islington out of my way. I see none yet dressed like her: I must look for a shag ruff, a frieze jerkin, a short sword, and a safeguard, or I get none."

If Moll does not show up, Laxton does not get laid.

Laxton continued saying to himself:

"Why, Moll, please make haste or the coachman will curse us soon."

Moll Cutpurse, fully dressed like a man, entered the scene.

Looking at Laxton, Moll said to herself:

"Oh, here's my gentleman. If they would keep their days as well with their mercers as their hours with their harlots, no bankrupt would give seven score pounds for a sergeant's place, for if you would know a catchpole rightly derived, the corruption of a citizen is the generation of a sergeant!"

Mercers are dealers in costly fabrics.

Where do catchpoles — sergeants who arrest people for debt — come from? A gentleman does not pay his debts, with the result that a shopkeeper goes bankrupt and becomes a catchpole. Because so many shopkeepers go bankrupt and become catchpoles, the price for becoming a sergeant goes up.

If gentlemen paid their bills as assiduously as they keep assignations with women, however, no shopkeepers would go bankrupt and need to find another way to make a living. Also, it wouldn't make sense to pay to become a catchpole because there would be no debtors and no bankrupts to arrest.

"Corruption" and "generation" are alchemical terms and refer to the dissolution of a substance that is then changed into another substance. People become corrupt through taking bribes. A good citizen "dies" when as a sergeant he begins to take bribes.

A proverb stated, "A sergeant is the spawn of some decayed shopkeeper."

A "decayed" shopkeeper is a shopkeeper who has fallen on bad times.

"Corruption" can mean 1) "decomposition of a corpse," or 2) "graft."

Moll Cutpurse then said to herself:

"How his eye hawks for venery!"

Laxton's eyes hunt for game — for women.

She then said to Laxton:

"Come, are you ready, sir?"

Not recognizing Moll, who was fully dressed as a man, Laxton said, "Ready for what, sir?"

"Do you ask that now, sir?" Moll Cutpurse said. "Why was this meeting appointed?"

Laxton said:

"I thought you mistook me, sir. You seem to be some young barrister."

"I have no suit in law; all my land's sold. I praise heaven for it; it has rid me of much trouble."

"Then I must wake you, sir," Moll said. "Where stands the coach?"

"Who's this?" Laxton asked. "Moll? Honest Moll?"

"So young and purblind — thoroughly blind?" Moll Cutpurse said. "You're an old wanton in your eyes, I see that."

Moll Cutpurse was implying that venereal disease had made Laxton blind.

"Thou are admirably suited for the Three Pigeons Inn at Brainford," Laxton said. "I'll swear I didn't know thee."

"I'll swear you did not, but you shall know me now," Moll Cutpurse said.

Laxton wanted to Biblically "know" her.

"No, not here, we shall be spied, indeed," Laxton said. "The coach is better. Come."

Coaches at this time contained a bed and had curtains over the windows.

"Wait," Moll said.

"What!" Laxton said. "Will thou untruss a point, Moll?"

"Untruss a point" means "undo a lace of clothing." Laxton thought Moll was eager to get undressed.

She took off her hat and cloak and drew her sword.

"Yes, here's the point that I untruss," Moll Cutpurse said. "It has but one tag; it will serve, though, to tie up a rogue's tongue."

The one tag was the hanger from which the sword had hung.

She had unsheathed her sword.

A tag is the metal tip of a lace that will be inserted into an eye-hole. Think of shoelaces, although these days the tip is usually plastic.

Moll was threatening to stab the point of her sword through Laxton's tongue.

What!" Laxton said.

Moll Cutpurse said:

"There's the gold with which you hired your hackney."

She gave him the ten gold angels that he had previously given to her.

She then threatened him with her sword and said:

"Here's her pace. She racks hard, and perhaps your bones will feel it!"

"Pace" and "rack" refer to the gait of a horse.

The rack was a medieval torture device on which the victim's body and joints were stretched.

Moll Cutpurse continued:

"Ten angels of my own I've put to thine.

"Win them and wear them!"

Often, the words "win her and wear her" referred to a bride. Make her your bride and enjoy her. In the case of a bride, "enjoy her" meant: sleep with her.

Moll was challenging Laxton to a winner-takes-all duel.

"Stop, Moll, Mistress Mary!" Laxton said.

"Draw, or I'll serve an execution on thee that shall lay thee up till doomsday!" Moll Cutpurse said.

The execution can be 1) the delivery of a legal writ accusing him of a crime, 2) capital punishment, and 3) performance of the sexual act.

A sword can be drawn, and in the slang of the time, so can a penis.

"Doomsday" is the Day of Judgment. "Lay him up until Doomsday" means that she will kill him.

"Draw upon a woman?" Laxton said. "Why, what do thou mean, Moll?"

Moll Cutpurse replied:

"I mean to teach thy base thoughts manners.

"Thou are one of those who think that each woman is thy fond and foolish, flexible and manageable whore if she just casts a liberal eye upon thee."

"Liberal" can mean 1) lustful, or 2) generous.

Moll continued:

"If she just turns back her head, she's thine, or among company, if she just by chance drinks first to thee. Then she's quite gone.

"There's no means to help her, nay, for a need — if thou feel like it — thou will swear unto thy credulous fellow lechers that thou are more in favor with a lady at first sight than her pet monkey all her lifetime.

"How many of our female sex by such as thou have their good thoughts repaid with a blasted name — a ruined reputation — who never deserved loosely, or did trip in the path of whoredom beyond cup and lip — between drinking to a man and kissing a man?"

A proverb stated, "There's many a slip between cup and lip."

Moll continued:

"Except for the stain of conscience and of soul, it would be better if women had fallen into the hands of a silent act than a bragging nothing."

"A silent act" would be an act of sex that is not talked about. "A bragging nothing" is telling without kissing — or anything beyond kissing.

Moll continued:

"There's no mercy in it. What dared move you, sir, to think me whorish, a name that I'd tear out from the high German's throat if it lay ledger — if it were recorded — there to dispatch privy — secret — slanders against me?"

In other words: If the high German lied in his throat that Moll Cutpurse was a whore, she would become Moll Cutthroat.

The high German was a tall German fencer.

Moll continued:

"In defying thee, I defy, challenge, and reject all men, their worst hates and their best flatteries, all their golden witchcrafts and charms with which they entangle the poor spirits of foolish women, distressed needlewomen, and trade-fallen wives."

This kind of entanglement could lead to Hell.

Trade-fallen wives were the wives of men whose businesses were failing or had fallen.

Moll continued:

"Fish that must necessarily bite or themselves be bitten — such hungry things as these may soon be taken with a worm fastened on a golden hook."

In the slang of this time, "fish" meant "woman" or "prostitute."

Moll continued:

"Those are the lecher's food, his prey; he watches for quarrelling wedlocks and poor shifting sisters — quarreling wives and poor prostitutes who shift beds and other women who have to shift for themselves to get food, clothing, and shelter — it is the best fish he takes.

"But why, good fisherman, am I thought to be meat for you, who never yet had an angling rod cast towards me?

"Because, you'll say, I'm given to sport and I'm playful: I'm often merry and I often jest.

"Had mirth no kindred — no friends and relatives — in the world but lust?

"Oh, shame may take all her friends then! But however thou and the baser world censure my life, I'll send them word by thee, and write with my sword so much upon thy breast, so that thou shall bear it in mind.

"Tell them — your future victims — it would be base to yield where I have conquered."

"Write [...] so much upon thy breast" is something that Lisbeth Salander, the protagonist of the novel *The Girl with a Dragon Tattoo* did. After she was raped, she set a trap for her rapist and tattooed on his chest the words "I AM A SADISTIC PIG, A PERVERT, AND A RAPIST."

Moll continued:

"I scorn to prostitute myself to a man, I who can prostitute a man to me, and so I greet and accost thee."

"Listen to me!" Laxton said.

"I wish that the spirits of all my slanderers were clasped in thine so that I might vex an army at one time!" Moll Cutpurse said.

They fought, and Moll wounded Laxton.

"I repent!" Laxton said. "Stop!"

"You'll die the better Christian then," Moll said.

Repenting makes a better Christian.

"I confess I have wronged thee, Moll," Laxton said.

"Confession is but poor amends for wrong, unless a rope to hang you would follow," Moll Cutpurse said.

This kind of confession is made by a criminal before the criminal is hanged.

"I ask thee for your pardon," Laxton said.

"I'm your hired whore, sir," Moll said.

Or so Laxton had thought, and so, he owed her.

"I yield both purse and body!" Laxton said.

Moll had won the gold angels.

"Both are mine and now at my disposal," Moll said.

"Spare my life!" Laxton pleaded.

"I scorn to strike thee basely," Moll said.

His sword was lowered in submission.

Laxton said:

"Spoken like a noble girl indeed!"

He said to himself:

"By God's heart, I think I fight with a familiar or the ghost of a fencer!"

Familiars were spirits that served witches.

Laxton continued saying to himself:

"She has wounded me gallantly — excellently and in the manner of a gallant.

"Call you this a lecherous voyage?"

He had hoped for a sexual liaison.

Laxton continued saying to himself:

"Here's blood that would have served me seven years in broken — cut-open — heads and cut fingers, and it now runs all out at once.

"A pox on the Three Pigeons Inn! I wish the coach were here now to carry me to the chirurgeon's."

A "chirurgeon" is a "surgeon."

Laxton exited, leaving the gold angels in Moll's possession.

Alone, Moll Cutpurse said to herself:

"If I could meet my enemies one by one thus, I might make pretty shift — good work — and deal handily with them in time and make them know that she who has wit and spirit may scorn to live beholden to her body for meat and food or for apparel like your common dame — whore — who makes shame to get clothes for her to cover the shame of her nakedness.

"Base is that mind that kneels unto her body, as if a husband stood in awe of his wife."

In Elizabethan and Jacobean England, a good wife was an obedient wife.

Moll Cutpurse continued:

"My spirit shall be mistress of this house — my body — as long as I have time in it."

Trapdoor entered the scene.

Seeing him, Moll Cutpurse said to herself:

"Oh, here comes the man who would be my serving-man. It is his hour — the time we agreed upon.

"Indeed, he is a good well-built fellow, if his spirit is similar to his umbles — his physical body. He walks stiffly — resolutely — but whether he will stand to it stiffly, there's the point."

Hmm. "Stand to it stiffly." Say no more.

Moll continued saying to herself:

"He has a good calf for it, and many a woman chooses the man she means to make her head — her husband — by his calf.

"I do not know their tricks and knacks in it. I don't know how they — the women — do it.

"Truly, he seems to be a man in his outside appearance; I'll test what he is inside."

Trapdoor said to himself:

"She told me Gray's Inn Fields between three and four.

"I'll fit her mistress-ship with a piece of service!"

The "piece" could be below his belly button, and he could "fit" it in her and service her.

Trapdoor continued saying to himself:

"I'm hired to rid the town of one mad girl."

Moll walked into and jostled him.

Trapdoor asked:

"What a pox ails you, sir?"

Moll said to herself, "He begins like a gentleman."

A gentleman will stand up for himself.

Trapdoor said:

"By God's heart, is the field so narrow, or your eyesight?"

Moll walked towards him.

Trapdoor said:

"By God's life, he comes back again!"

"Was this spoken to me, sir?" Moll Cutpurse asked.

"I cannot tell, sir," Trapdoor said.

"Go to; you are a coxcomb!" Moll said. "You are a fool!"

"Go to" can mean "go to hell!"

"Coxcomb?" Trapdoor said.

"You are a slave!" Moll said.

"I hope there's law for you, sir," Trapdoor said.

He hoped a police officer would arrest "him" — he thought that Moll was a rude man.

"Yea, do you see, sir?" Moll said.

She turned his hat.

This was an insult.

Trapdoor said:

"By God's heart, this is no good dealing!"

"Please let me know what house you're of."

"One of the Temple, sir," Moll said.

Moll meant a lawyer. The Inner Temple and the Middle Temple were two Inns of Court.

She flicked him with her finger.

This was another insult.

"By the mass, so I think!" Trapdoor said.

"And yet sometimes I lie about — live in — Chick Lane," Moll said.

Chick Lane was known to be infested with criminals.

"I like you the worse because you shift your lodging so often," Trapdoor said. "I'll not meddle with you because of that trick, sir."

He did not want to fight either a lawyer (resident of the Temple) or a hardened criminal (resident of Chick Lane).

"A good shift, but it shall not serve your turn," Moll Cutpurse said. "A good evasion, but it won't help you."

"You'll allow me to go about my business, sir?" Trapdoor asked.

"Your business?" Moll Cutpurse said. "I'll make you wait on me before I have done, and I'll make you glad to serve me, too."

"What, sir! Serve you?" Trapdoor said. "Not if there were no more men in England!"

"But if there were no more women in England, I hope you'd wait upon your mistress then," Moll said.

"Mistress!" Trapdoor said.

He now recognized her.

"Oh, you're a tried spirit at a push, sir!" Moll said.

"At a push" means "when push comes to shove," but "pushing" is also done during sex.

A "tried spirit" is an "experienced fighter."

"What would your worship have me do?" Trapdoor asked.

"Are you a fighter?" Moll asked.

"No, I praise heaven," Trapdoor said. "I had better grace and more manners."

"As how, I ask, sir?" Moll asked.

"By God's life, it had been a beastly part — a beastly act — of me to have drawn my weapons upon my mistress!" Trapdoor said. "All the world would have bitterly reproached me for that."

His "mistress" was Moll: the woman he would work for.

"Weapons." Plural. Hmm. One weapon was his sword.

"Why, but you didn't know me," Moll Cutpurse said.

"Do not say so, mistress," Trapdoor said. "I knew you by your wide straddle, as well as if I had been in your belly."

Moll Cutpurse habitually stood with her legs far apart.

Rocker Suzi Quatro had a similar stance. She performed her rock and roll while wearing a leather jumpsuit — a sexy outfit that helped many teenaged boys get through puberty — and her mother once told her that her music was "very nice, but do you have to stand with your legs so far apart?"

"As well as if I had been in your belly." Hmm. Close, but more specifically what he really meant was "as well as if I had been in your vagina."

"Well, we shall try you further," Moll said. "In the meantime we give you entertainment — we employ you."

"I thank your good mistress-ship," Trapdoor said.

"How many suits of clothing do you have?" Moll asked.

"I have no more suits than I have backs, mistress," Trapdoor said.

"Well, if you deserve it, next week I will cast off this suit of clothing I am wearing, and you may creep into it and wear it as yours," Moll said.

"I thank your good worship," Trapdoor said.

"Come, follow me to St. Thomas Apostle's," Moll said. "I'll put a livery cloak upon your back the first thing I do."

St. Thomas Apostle's was a church.

"Livery" was distinctive clothing that showed for whom a servant worked.

"I follow, my dear mistress," Trapdoor said.

They exited.

— 3.2 —

In Gallipot's house, the Gallipots had just finished eating.

Mistress Gallipot entered a room, and her husband followed her. He was upset because she had left the dining table and their guests.

"What are you doing, Pru!" Gallipot said. "Nay, sweet Prudence!"

Mistress Prudence Gallipot said:

"What a pruing do you keep up! I think the baby would have a teat, it kyes — it cries — so."

She was speaking baby-talk to her husband.

Mistress Gallipot continued:

"Please don't be so fond of me; leave your city humors and city moods. I'm vexed at you to see how like a calf you come bleating after me."

City husbands were reputed to be subservient to their wives.

A "calf" is a fool.

"Nay, honey Pru," Gallipot said. "How does your rising up before all the dinner guests look? And departing so abruptly from my friends so uncivilly? Bah, Pru, bah, come!"

"Come" can mean "cum."

"Then up and ride, indeed," Mistress Gallipot said.

Hmm. "Up and ride." Say no more.

"Up and ride?" Gallipot said. "Nay, my pretty Pru, that's far from my thought, duck. Why, mouse, thy mind is nibbling at something. Whatever is it? What has upset thy stomach?"

"Such an ass as you," Mistress Gallipot said. "Heyday, you had best turn midwife or physician! You are an apothecary already, but I'm not one of your drugs — or your drudges."

"Thou are a sweet drug, sweetest Pru, and the more thou are pounded, the more precious," Gallipot said.

"Pounded" can happen 1) in a mortar and with a pestle, or 2) in bed.

"Must you be prying into a woman's secrets?" Mistress Gallipot asked. "What do you say?"

A woman's secrets include her private parts.

"Woman's secrets?" Gallipot said.

76

"What!" Mistress Gallipot said. "I cannot have a qualm of nausea come upon me but your teeth water — your mouth waters — until your nose hangs over it."

His mouth waters until he can stick his nose in her business.

"It is my love for you, dear wife," Gallipot said.

Mistress Gallipot said:

"Your love? Your love is all words; give me deeds."

A proverb stated, "From words to deeds is a great space."

Mistress Gallipot continued:

"I cannot abide a man who is too fond and foolish over me, so cookish; thou do not know how to handle a woman in her kind — as she deserves."

"Cookish" means "like a cook" — always hovering over the food or other object, such as a wife.

"No, Pru?" Gallipot said. "Why, I hope I have handled —"

Mistress Gallipot interrupted, "— handle a fool's head of your own! Bah! Bah!"

Fools carried a baton or bauble, at the end of which was a fool's head. The baton or bauble was sometimes compared to a dildo.

A fool's head could be the head of Gallipot's penis.

"Ha, ha! It is such a wasp!" Gallipot said. "It does me good now to have her sting me, little rogue."

The word "sting" can mean "sexually arouse."

"Now, bah!" Mistress Gallipot said. "How you vex me! I cannot abide these apron-husbands who are such cotqueans. You overdo your things; they become you scurvily."

"Apron-husbands" are husbands who are tied to their wife's apron strings.

"Cotqueans" are husbands who meddle in their wife's affairs.

Gallipot said to himself:

"Upon my life, she breeds!"

Pregnant women were thought to be difficult.

Gallipot continued saying to himself:

"Heaven knows how I have strained myself to please her, night and day. I wonder why we citizens should beget children so fretful and untoward and difficult to manage in the breeding, their fathers being for the most part as gentle as milch-kine — as milk-cows."

He then said out loud:

"Shall I leave thee, my Pru?"

"Bah! Bah! Bah!" Mistress Gallipot said.

"Thou shall be vexed no more, pretty, kind rogue," Gallipot said. "Take no cold, sweet Pru."

"Take no cold" means 1) don't catch cold, and/or 2) don't become depressed.

Gallipot exited.

Alone, Mistress Gallipot said to herself:

"As your wit has done — it has taken cold."

She took out a letter.

This was why she had left the dining table: to read the letter in private.

She continued saying to herself:

"Now, Master Laxton, show your head. What is the news from you? Would any husband suspect that a woman crying, 'Buy my scurvygrass,' should bring love letters among her herbs to his wife?"

That was how she had received Laxton's letter.

"Scurvygrass" is a vegetable that was reputed to stop the disease scurvy.

"Show your head" can mean 1) tell me what you are thinking, or 2) show me the head of your penis.

Mistress Gallipot continued saying to herself:

"A pretty trick and deception! A fine conveyance and delivery of letters! Had jealousy and suspicion a thousand eyes, a silly, innocent woman with scurvygrass blinds them all."

In mythology, Argos was a giant with a thousand eyes. Hera, the jealous wife of Zeus, king of the gods, commanded Argos to watch Io, a woman whom her husband wanted to sleep with, but Zeus sent Hermes to make Argus fall asleep, and then Hermes killed him.

Mistress Gallipot continued saying to herself:

"Laxton, with bay laurel leaves I crown thy wit for this. It deserves praise."

Celebrated poets, athletes, and generals were crowned with laurel leaves.

Mistress Gallipot continued saying to herself:

"This makes me affect and love thee more; this proves thee wise.

"Alas, what poor shift and trick is love forced to devise?

"Now, to get to the point."

Alone, Mistress Gallipot read the letter out loud:

"*'Oh, sweet creature,'* — a sweet beginning — *'pardon my long absence, for thou shall shortly be possessed with my presence. Though Demophon was false to Phyllis, I will be to thee as Pan-da-rus was to Cres-sida; although Aeneas made an ass of Dido, I will die to thee before I do so.'*"

Demophon, one of Theseus' sons, married Phyllis, a Bisaltian princess, after the Trojan War. Tiring of her, he left her, using the excuse that he wanted to visit Athens, his home, and promising to return at the end of a year. She knew that he would not return to her, and she gave him a casket and told him to open it when he despaired of ever returning to her. Instead of going home, he went to Cyprus. At the end of a year, Demophon had not returned to her, and she committed suicide. Demophon opened the casket, and its contents, whatever they were, made him insane. Furiously riding his horse, he was thrown off and impaled on his own sword and died.

During the Trojan War, Pandarus was a go-between between Cressida and Troilus, who had an affair but never married. From the name "Pandarus," we get the word "pandar." Pandarus never slept with Cressida, who was his niece. Cressida eventually became the mistress of the Greek warrior Diomedes.

Laxton has never slept with Mistress Gallipot, and if he were to treat her the way that Pandarus treated Cressida, he would be her pimp, not her lover.

Mistress Gallipot sounded out the names "Pan-da-rus" and "Cres-sida" as if they were unfamiliar to her. This helped the audience to hear and recognize the names. If she had said the names quickly, the audience may have thought only of Troilus and Cressida and not have thought about why she mentioned Pandarus.

After the Trojan War, Aeneas had a famous affair with Dido, Queen of Carthage. He left her so he could fulfill his destiny of going to Italy and becoming an important ancestor of the Romans. Because she had been abandoned by Aeneas, Dido committed suicide.

The word "die" can mean "have an orgasm."

Mistress Gallipot continued to read the letter out loud:

"*'Oh, sweetest creature, make much of me, for no man beneath the silver moon shall make more of a woman than I do of thee.'*"

Laxton hoped to make more *from* the woman who is Mistress Gallipot. She was thinking of romance; he was thinking of money.

Mistress Gallipot continued to read the letter out loud:

"'*Furnish me therefore with thirty pounds; you must do it of necessity for me. I languish until I see some comfort come from thee, protesting not to die in thy debt, but rather to live so, as hitherto I have and will.*'"

He did not want to die in her debt, but rather to live in her debt — to owe money to her his entire life.

Mistress Gallipot finished reading the letter out loud:

"'*Thy true Laxton ever.*'"

Mistress Gallipot said to herself:

"Alas, poor gentleman! Truly, I pity him.

"How shall I raise this money? Thirty pounds?

"It is thirty, to be sure, a 3 before an O."

Turn the 3 to the right on its side, and it represents a pair of testicles. The O represents a vagina. So 30 is a pair of testicles very close to a vagina.

Mistress Gallipot continued saying to herself:

"I know his threes too well."

Hmm. Maybe in her daydreams.

Mistress Gallipot continued saying to herself:

"My childbed linen? Shall I pawn that for him? Then if my mark becomes known, I am undone and ruined; it may be thought that my husband's bankrupt."

Childbed linen was expensive linen for use during confinement due to pregnancy and childbirth. The mark was embroidery that identified who had ordered these items to be made.

Mistress Gallipot continued saying to herself:

"Which way shall I turn?

"Laxton, what with my own fears and thy wants, I'm like a needle between two adamants."

Adamants are magnets: lodestones. Mistress Gallipot was between a rock and a hard place.

Master Gallipot entered the scene hastily.

He said:

"Nay, nay, wife, the women are all up!"

The women had left the table and had gone into another room, leaving the men by themselves to smoke, drink, and talk together. As the hostess, Mistress Gallipot should be with the women.

Seeing her holding a letter, he said to himself:

"Ha! What! Reading letters? I smell a goose, a couple of capons, and a gammon of bacon from her mother out of the country, I bet my life.

"Steal! Steal!"

He wanted to steal close behind her and read the letter, which he thought was about his wife's mother sending them food from the country. Or he wanted to steal the letter from her hands and read it.

"Oh, beshrew your heart!" Mistress Gallipot said, noticing him.

"What letter's that?" Gallipot said. "I'll see it."

She tore the letter into pieces.

"Oh, I wish that thou had no eyes to see the downfall of me and thyself," Mistress Gallipot said. "I'm undone, forever! Forever!"

"What ails my Pru?" Gallipot said. "What paper is that which thou tear?"

"I wish that I could tear my very heart in pieces, for my soul lies on the rack of shame that tortures me beyond a woman's suffering," Mistress Gallipot said.

"What is the meaning of this?" Gallipot asked.

Mistress Gallipot said, "Had you [fate, or the gods] no other vengeance to throw down but even in height of all my joys —"

Gallipot interrupted, "Dear woman!"

Mistress Gallipot continued, "— when the full sea of pleasure and content seemed to flow over me."

Gallipot said, "As thou desire to keep me out of Bedlam, tell me what troubles thee? Has thy child at nurse fallen sick or dead?"

Bedlam was an insane asylum.

The child was with a wet-nurse. A wet nurse suckles an infant for the mother.

"Oh, no!" Mistress Gallipot said.

"Heavens bless me!" Gallipot said. "Are my barns and houses yonder at Hockley Hole consumed with fire? I can build more, sweet Pru."

"It is worse," Mistress Gallipot said. "It is worse."

"Has my factor — my agent — broke and become bankrupt, or has the *Jonas* sunk?" Gallipot asked.

In the Bible, the prophet Jonas was thrown overboard in a storm and he was swallowed by a whale.

Gallipot had invested in the *Jonas* or its cargo.

"I wish that all we had were swallowed in the waves, rather than we both should be the scorn of slaves — the laughingstock of lower-class people," Mistress Gallipot said.

"I'm at my wits' end!" Gallipot said.

Mistress Gallipot said:

"Oh, my dear husband, whereas once I thought myself a fixed star placed only in the heaven of thine arms, I fear now I shall prove a wanderer."

The North star — Polaris — always seems to be in the same place in the night sky, and so it is a symbol of a constant, loyal, chaste person. The wandering stars are planets that seem to wander in the night sky.

She continued:

"Oh, Laxton, Laxton, is it then my fate to be by thee overthrown?"

Gallipot said:

"Prevent me, wisdom, from falling into frenzy and insanity!"

He knelt in supplication and said:

"On my knees, sweet Pru, speak. Who is that Laxton who so heavy lies on thy bosom?"

"So heavy lies on thy bosom" figuratively means "disturbs you." Literally, it has a bawdy meaning.

"I shall surely run mad!" Mistress Gallipot said.

Gallipot said:

"I shall run mad for company — run mad along with thee — then.

"Speak to me: I'm Gallipot, thy husband.

"Pru, why, Pru! Are thou sick in conscience for some villainous deed thou were about to enact? Did thou mean to rob me?"

She did mean to rob him. She wanted to give 30 pounds to Laxton.

Gallipot continued:

"Tush, I forgive thee! Have thou on my bed thrust my soft pillow under another's head? I'll wink at and overlook all thy faults, Pru. Alas, that's no more than what some neighbors near thee have done before.

"Sweet honey Pru, who's that Laxton?"

"Oh!" Mistress Gallipot said.

"Out with him!" Gallipot said. "Tell me about him!"

Mistress Gallipot said:

"Oh, he's born to be my undoer!

"This hand that thou call thine was given to him. To him I was made sure — I was betrothed — in the sight of heaven."

If this were true (it was not), it would be an impediment to her marriage to Gallipot.

"I never heard this thunder," Gallipot said.

Mistress Gallipot said:

"Yes, yes, before I was to thee contracted, to him I swore, since last I saw him twelve months three times told the moon has drawn through her light silver bow."

This was a fancy way of saying this: Since I last saw him three years ago.

She was making up a story, and she used fancy language and rhyme to tell it. If she were not making up a story, she would most likely use plain language.

If the story were true, and if she had been legally contracted to marry Laxton before she married Gallipot, that could bring the legality of her marriage to Gallipot into question.

Mistress Gallipot continued:

"For over the seas he went, and it was said,

"But rumor lies, that he in France was dead.

"But he's alive! Oh, he's alive! He sent

"That letter to me, which in rage I rent,

"Swearing with oaths most damnably to have me ...

"Or tear me from the bosom of my husband.

"Oh, may the heavens save me!"

"My heart will break!" Gallipot said. "Shamed and undone and ruined forever!"

Mistress Gallipot said, "So black a day, poor wretch, went over thee never."

Gallipot said:

"If thou should wrestle with him at the law, thou are sure to fall. No odd sleight or trick can help you, no contrivance can help you, no prevention can help you."

In other words: If Laxton sued, he would win the lawsuit. If he won the lawsuit, he would be the man married to Mistress Gallipot and so she would be Mistress Laxton.

Gallipot then said:

"I'll tell him thou are with child."

If she were pregnant with another man's child, Laxton probably would not want to be married to her.

Mistress Gallipot said, "Umm."

She was not happy with this.

Gallipot continued:

"Or I will give out that one of my men was taken in bed with thee."

If she were a known adulteress, Laxton probably would not want to be married to her.

"Umm, umm," Mistress Gallipot said.

She was very much not happy with this: This would ruin her reputation.

"Before I lose thee, my dear Pru," Gallipot said. "I'll drive it to that push — to that extremity. I will take it that far."

"Worse, and worse still," Mistress Gallipot said. "You embrace a mischief to prevent an ill."

In this society, the word "mischief" had a strong meaning: evil.

"I'll buy thee from him," Gallipot said. "I'll stop his mouth with gold. Do thou think that it will do?"

Mistress Gallipot, who wanted to give Laxton 30 pounds, said:

"Oh, me! May the heavens grant it would!

"Yet now my senses are set more in tune. He wrote, as I remember in his letter, that he in riding up and down while looking for me, had spent thirty pounds before he could find me.

"Send that. Don't stand on thirty pounds with him. Don't resist giving him the money."

Gallipot said:

"Forty, Pru.

"Say thou the word — it is done. We venture and risk lives for wealth, but we must do more to keep our wives.

"Thirty or forty, Pru?"

"Thirty pounds, good sweet," Mistress Gallipot said. "Of an ill bargain let's save what we can. I'll pay it to him with my tears: When first I knew him, he was a man of a meek spirit. All goodness is not yet dried up, I hope."

Gallipot said:

"He shall have thirty pounds; let that stop all.

"Love's sweets taste best when we have drunk down gall."

Tiltyard and Mistress Tiltyard, Goshawk, and Mistress Openwork entered the scene.

Seeing them, Gallipot said:

"God-so, our friends!"

He said to his wife:

"Come, come, smooth your cheek. After a storm, the face of heaven looks sleek and tranquil."

"God-so" is an oath. It may mean "By God's soul."

"Didn't I tell you these turtledoves were together?" Tiltyard said.

Turtledoves are lovebirds.

Mistress Tiltyard said to Mistress Gallipot, "How are thou doing, sirrah? Why, sister Gallipot!"

The word "sirrah" could be used to address a female friend.

The word "sister" was not meant literally. It could be used to address a female friend.

"Lord, how she's changed!" Mistress Openwork said.

"Is your wife ill, sir?" Goshawk asked Gallipot.

"Yes, indeed, la, sir, very ill, very ill, never worse!" Gallipot said.

Mistress Tiltyard felt Mistress Gallipot's forehead and said, "How her head burns! Feel how her pulses work."

"Sister, lie down a little," Mistress Openwork said. "That always does me good."

Women can lie down for a purpose other than rest and recuperation.

"In good seriousness, I find best ease in that, too," Mistress Tiltyard said. "Has she laid some hot thing to her stomach?"

"Some hot thing" means "medicine" or something with a medical purpose, but of course, the phrase has a bawdy meaning.

"No, but I will lay something soon," Mistress Gallipot said.

"Come, come, fools, you trouble her," Tiltyard said. "Shall we go, Master Goshawk?"

Goshawk said:

"Yes, sweet Master Tiltyard."

Taking Mistress Rosamond Openwork aside, he said quietly to her:

"Sirrah Rosamond, I bet my life Gallipot has vexed his wife."

"She has a horrible high color indeed," Mistress Openwork said. "Her face is flushed."

"We shall have your face painted with the same red soon at night when your husband comes from his rubbers in a false alley," Goshawk said. "Thou will not believe me that his bowls run with a wrong bias."

Using terminology from the game of bowls, Goshawk was trying to convince Mistress Openwork that her husband was having an affair. This was part of his plotting to sleep with her.

The word "rubbers" is often singular. It can be 1) the third game in a set of three games, and/or 2) the woman whom Openwork is supposed to be sexually rubbing.

An "alley" is an undulation in the ground the game is played on. A "false alley" is a vagina that Openwork ought not to Biblically know.

"Bowls" are "balls." Openwork has testicles.

"Bias" is an oblique rolling of the ball. Openwork was biased in favor of his supposed partner in adultery. So said Goshawk.

Mistress Openwork said, "It cannot sink into me that he feeds upon stale mutton abroad, despite having better and fresher mutton at home."

"Mutton" usually means a harlot; "stale mutton" means a worn-out harlot. But Mistress Openwork was saying her husband had fresher "mutton" — she herself — at home.

"Abroad" means "outside the home."

"What if I bring thee where thou shall see him stand at rack and manger?" Goshawk asked.

"Rack and manger" means "an abundance of food." Here, it means "an abundance of 'mutton.'"

A "stand" can be a penile erection.

"I'll saddle him in his kind and spur him until he kicks again," Mistress Openwork said.

She would subdue him and treat him as he ought to be treated. Or she would have rough sex with him.

"Shall thou and I ride our journey then?" Goshawk asked.

This meant: Shall I take you where you can see your husband and his "mutton"?

He also meant: Shall we have an affair?

"Here's my hand," Mistress Openwork said.

Goshawk said quietly to her:

"No more."

He then said out loud:

"Come, Master Tiltyard, shall we leap into the stirrups with our women and amble home?"

"Amble" is a particular gait of a horse.

The word "riding" is frequently used when referring to sex.

"Yes, yes," Tiltyard said. "Come, wife."

"In truth, sister, I hope you will do well for all this," Mistress Tiltyard said.

Mistress Gallipot said:

"I hope I shall.

"Farewell, good sister, sweet Master Goshawk."

"Welcome, brother, most kindly welcome, sir," Goshawk said.

"Thanks, sir, for our good cheer," one of the leave-takers said.

Everyone except Gallipot and his wife exited.

Gallipot said to his wife, continuing their discussion about giving Laxton 30 pounds:

"It shall be so, so that a crafty knave shall not outreach and outwit me nor walk by my door with my wife arm in arm, as if she were his whore.

"I'll give him a golden coxcomb: thirty pounds.

"Tush, Pru, what's thirty pounds? Sweet duck, look cheerfully."

"Thou are worthy of my heart," Mistress Gallipot said. "Thou buy it dearly."

Laxton entered the scene. His face was muffled: He had partially covered it so he would not be recognized.

Laxton was hiding his face perhaps because he had to hide from creditors: Moll Cutpurse had taken his ten gold angels. Also, when doing something unethical, few people want to be recognized.

Laxton said to himself:

"By God's light, the tide's against me!"

He had not expected to see Gallipot — just Mistress Gallipot.

Laxton said to himself about Gallipot:

"A pox of your apothecaryship! Oh, for some glister — an enema — to set him going!"

He then said to himself:

"It is one of Hercules' labors to tread — have sex with — one of these city hens because their cocks are always crowing over them.

"There's no turning tail here, I must go on."

Hercules performed twelve famous labors as penance for killing his wife and children in a fit of insanity.

"Tail" can mean "cunt."

Seeing Laxton, Mistress Gallipot said, "Oh, husband, look! He comes!"

"Let me deal with him," Gallipot said.

"Bless you, sir," Laxton said.

"Be you blessed, too, sir, if you come in peace," Gallipot said.

"Do you have any good pudding tobacco, sir?" Laxton said.

"Pudding" is sausage. "Pudding tobacco" is compressed tobacco that is shaped so that it resembles a sausage.

Laxton may have been asking: Do you have a good "sausage" between your legs? Are you a real man? Do you have courage?

Mistress Gallipot said:

"Oh, pick no quarrels, gentle sir! My husband is not a man of weapons as you are.

"He knows everything: I have opened all before him concerning you. I have told him everything."

"By God's wounds, has she shown him my letters!" Laxton said to himself.

Mistress Gallipot said:

"Suppose my case were yours, what would you do at such a pinch, such batteries, such assaults of father, mother, kindred, to dissolve the knot you tied, and to be bound to him?

"How could you shift this storm off?"

"Suppose my case were yours" can mean "suppose my vagina were yours."

Mistress Gallipot was cleverly informing Laxton about the lie she had told her husband: the lie that she had been betrothed to him.

She was also lying that a barrage of protests from her family members had made her break her contract with Laxton so that she would marry Gallipot and not Laxton.

"If I know, hang me," Laxton said.

He did not yet know what was going on.

Mistress Gallipot said, "Besides, a story of your death was read each minute to me."

"What a pox does this riddling mean?" Laxton said to himself.

Gallipot said:

"Be wise, sir. Let's you and I not be tossed and bandied on lawyers' pens. They have sharp nibs and draw men's very heart-blood from them.

"What need do you have, sir, to beat the drum of and make public my wife's infamy, and call your friends together, sir, to prove your precontract of marriage when she has confessed it?"

"Umm, sir, has she confessed it?" Laxton asked.

He was beginning to understand.

"She has confessed it, indeed, to me, sir, after receiving your letter that was sent to her," Gallipot said.

"I have," Mistress Gallipot said. "I have."

Laxton said to himself:

"If I let this iron cool, call me a slave."

A proverb stated, "Strike while the iron is hot."

He then said out loud:

"Do you hear, you dame Prudence? Do thou think, vile woman, I'll take these blows and wink and do nothing?"

Mistress Gallipot knelt and began, "Upon my knees —"

Pretending to be angry at her, Laxton interrupted, "Out, impudence!"

Gallipot began, "Good sir —"

"You goatish — lustful — slaves," Laxton said. "Had you no wild fowl to cut up but mine?"

In this society, "wild fowl" is slang for "whore" or "loose woman."

Laxton was complaining that Gallipot should have had a woman other than the one who was betrothed to him (Laxton) to sleep with.

"Alas, sir, you make her flesh tremble," Gallipot said. "Do not frighten her. She shall do what is reasonable and fitting."

"I'll have thee, even if thou were more common than a hospital and more diseased," Laxton said to Mistress Gallipot.

"Have thee" can mean 1) marry thee, and/or 2) have sex with thee.

"Common" means "open to all comers." Applied to a woman, the word means "whore."

"Let me say just one word, good sir," Gallipot said.

"What word, sir?" Laxton asked.

Gallipot said:

"I married her, have lain with her, and have begotten two children on her body; just think about that.

"Have you so beggarly an appetite, when I have fed upon a dainty dish, to dine upon my scraps, my leavings?

"Huh, sir? Do I come near you now, sir?"

"By our Lady, you touch me," Laxton said. "You make a good point."

"Wouldn't you scorn to wear my clothes, sir?" Gallipot asked.

Servants were sometimes given their masters' old clothing.

"That is right, sir," Laxton said.

"Then please, sir, do not wear her, for she's a garment so fitting for my body, I'm loath another should put it on; you will undo both.

"Your letter, she said, stated your complaint that you had spent some thirty pounds in quest of her: I'll pay it.

"Shall that, sir, stop this gap up between you two?"

Laxton said:

"Well, if I swallow this wrong that has been done to me, let her thank you.

"The money being paid, sir, I am gone.

"Farewell. Oh, women! Happy is he who trusts none."

"Dispatch him hence, sweet husband," Mistress Gallipot said. "Settle the matter and send him away."

Gallipot said:

"Yes, dear wife."

He said to Laxton:

"Please, sir, come in."

He then said to his wife:

"Before Master Laxton departs, thou shall in wine drink a toast to him."

This would be a gesture of goodwill.

Mistress Gallipot said:

"With all my heart."

She whispered to Laxton:

"How do thou like my wit?"

Laxton whispered back:

"Splendidly."

Master Gallipot exited.

Laxton said:

"That wile by which the serpent did the first woman beguile did ever since all women's bosoms fill."

Mistress Gallipot exited.

Alone, Laxton said to himself:

"You are apple-eaters all, deceivers still."

He was referring to Eve eating the fruit of the Tree of Knowledge in the Garden of Eden.

Laxton exited.

On Holborn Street, Sir Alexander Wengrave, Sir Davy Dapper, and Sir Adam Appleton saw Trapdoor nearby.

"Out with your tale, Sir Davy, to Sir Adam," Sir Alexander said. "A knave who is within my eyesight is deep in my debt."

This was his excuse to go over to and talk privately to Trapdoor.

"If he is a knave, sir, hold him fast," Sir Davy Dapper said.

Sir Alexander went over to Trapdoor.

"Speak softly," Sir Alexander said. "What egg is there hatching now?"

Trapdoor said:

"A duck's egg, sir, a duck that has eaten a frog."

In other words: Moll Cutpurse has taken or will soon take the bait.

Trapdoor continued:

"I have cracked the shell and some villainy or other will peep out soon. The duck that sits is the bouncing ramp —that roaring girl who is my mistress — and the drake that must tread her is your son Sebastian."

A "bouncing ramp" is a badly behaved woman: Moll Cutpurse.

"Tread" means "have sex with."

"Be quick —" Sir Alexander began.

"— as the tongue of an oyster-wench," Trapdoor interrupted.

Oyster-wenches sell oysters.

"And see that thy news is true—" Sir Alexander began.

Trapdoor interrupted:

"— as a barber's every Saturday night."

Barbers talk to a lot of people and hear a lot of gossip; not all of the gossip can be true.

Trapdoor continued:

"Mad Moll —"

"Ah," Sir Alexander said.

"— must be let in without knocking at your back gate," Trapdoor continued.

"So," Sir Alexander said.

"Your chamber will be made bawdy," Trapdoor said.

"Good," Sir Alexander said.

"She comes in a shirt of mail," Trapdoor said.

A shirt of mail can be chainmail.

"What!" Sir Alexander said. "A shirt of mail?"

"Yes, sir, or a male shirt, that's to say in man's apparel," Trapdoor said.

"To my son?" Sir Alexander asked.

Trapdoor said:

"Close to your son. Your son and her moon will be in conjunction if all almanacs don't lie."

"In conjunction" means "in the same zodiacal sign," but of course the phrase has a bawdy sense.

Trapdoor continued:

"Her black safeguard is turned into a deep Dutch slop, the holes of her upper body to button holes, her waistcoat to a doublet, her placket to the ancient seat of a codpiece, and you shall take them both — Moll and Sebastian — with standing collars."

"The holes of her upper body" are eyelets.

Feminine attire had eyelets, and male attire had buttons.

A "placket" is an opening in a petticoat.

A "standing collar" is a collar that stands high and upright.

In other words: Moll Cutpurse would be dressed entirely in men's clothing.

"Are thou sure of this?" Sir Alexander asked.

"As sure as every throng of people is sure of a pickpocket, as sure as a whore is of the clients all Michaelmas Term and of the pox after the term," Trapdoor said.

Michaelmas Term is a period of time in the legal year. Lots of lawyers and clients would have money to pay prostitutes. After the term was over, lots of people would find that they were infected with venereal disease.

"The time of their tilting?" Sir Alexander asked.

A "tilt" is a "joust."

The two were expected to engage in sexual jousting.

"Three," Trapdoor said.

"The day?" Sir Alexander asked.

"This," Trapdoor said.

"Away, ply it, do your job and watch her," Sir Alexander said.

"As the devil does for the death of a bawd, I'll watch her; you catch her," Trapdoor said.

"She's as good as caught," Sir Alexander said. "Here weave thou the nets. Listen —"

"They are made," Trapdoor interrupted. "The nets that will trap her are prepared."

"I told the other knights — Sir Adam and Sir Davy — thou did owe me money; hold the pretense up, maintain it," Sir Alexander said.

Trapdoor replied:

"Stiffly, as a Puritan does contention."

Puritans strenuously defended their religious beliefs.

He then said loudly so that Sir Davy Dapper and Sir Adam Appleton would hear:

"By the pox, I don't owe thee the value of a halfpenny halter!"

A halter is a hanging rope with a noose.

"Thou shall be hanged in it before thou escape so!" Sir Alexander said. "Varlet, I'll make thee look through a debtor's prison grate."

Trapdoor replied:

"I'll do it presently, through a tavern grate."

The tavern grate is the latticework that identified a tavern in this society.

Trapdoor called:

"Drawer! Tapster!"

He then said:

"Pish!"

Trapdoor exited.

"Has the knave vexed you, sir?" Sir Adam asked.

Sir Alexander said:

"I asked him for my money; he swears my son received it.

"Oh, that boy will never stop heaping sorrows on my heart until he has quite broken it."

"Is he still wild?" Sir Adam asked.

"As wild as a Russian bear," Sir Alexander replied.

Bears were imported from Russia and used in bear baitings. These bears were renowned for their ferocity.

"But has he left his old haunt with that baggage — that wanton woman?" Sir Adam asked. "That Moll?"

"He is worse still and worse," Sir Alexander said. "He lays on me his shame; I lay on him my curse."

"My son Jack Dapper then shall run with him, all in one pasture," Sir Davy Dapper said.

In other words: Sebastian and Jack Dapper will be in the same boat.

"Does your son prove to be bad, too, sir?" Sir Adam asked.

Sir Davy Dapper answered:

"As villainy can make him."

He then said to Sir Alexander:

"Your Sebastian dotes on just one drab, mine on a thousand."

He then mentioned other things that his son doted on:

"Noise — a band — of fiddlers, tobacco, wine, and a whore, a mercer who will let him buy more on credit, dice, and a water-spaniel with a duck.

"Oh, bring him a-bed with these!"

In other words: Let him be delivered from these things, just as a woman is delivered of a baby.

Or: Let him go to his sickbed and be cured of these things.

Sir Davy Dapper continued:

"When his purse jingles, roaring boys follow at his tale — its sound — fencers and ningles, which are beasts that Adam never gave a name to."

Genesis 2:19-20 states (King James Version):

19) And out of the ground the LORD God formed every beast of the field, and every fowl of the air; and brought them unto Adam to see what he would call them: and whatsoever Adam called every living creature, that was the name thereof.

20) And Adam gave names to all cattle, and to the fowl of the air, and to every beast of the field; but for Adam there was not found an help meet for him.

"Ningles" are "ingles": favorite friends and/or catamites. A catamite is a boy or young man who is kept for homosexual uses. Adam never gave a name to such creatures.

Sir Davy Dapper continued:

"These horse-leeches — parasites — suck my son; he being drawn dry, they all live on smoke."

"Tobacco?" Sir Alexander asked.

Sir Davy Dapper answered:

"Right, but I have in my brain a windmill going that shall grind to dust the follies of my son and make him wise or a stark fool."

He then said to Sir Alexander and Sir Adam:

"Please lend me your advice."

Sir Alexander and Sir Adam said, "That advice you shall get, good Sir Davy."

Sir Davy Dapper said:

"Here's the springe — the trap — I have set to catch this woodcock in."

A "woodcock" is literally an easily caught bird and figuratively a fool.

Sir Davy Dapper said:

"A legal action in a false name, unknown to him, has been entered in the counter to arrest my son: Jack Dapper."

A "counter" or "compter" is a debtors' prison.

Being arrested could convince Jack Dapper that he needed to reform his mode of life.

Sir Alexander and Sir Adam laughed.

"Do you think that the counter cannot break him?" Sir Davy Dapper asked.

"Break him?" Sir Adam said. "Yes, it can break him and break his heart, too, if he lies and stays there long."

"I'll make him sing a counter-tenor, to be sure," Sir Davy Dapper said.

"Counter-tenors" sing high notes.

Castrati sang counter-tenor parts.

"No way to tame him like it," Sir Adam said. "There he shall learn what money is indeed, and how to spend it."

"He's bridled there," Sir Davy Dapper said.

Bridewell was a prison for prostitutes.

Sir Alexander said:

"Aye, yet he doesn't know how to mend it.

"Bedlam does not cure more madmen in a year than one of the counters — the debtor prisons — does; men pay more dearly there for their wit than anywhere.

"A counter — why, it is a university! Who doesn't see that?

"As scholars there, so men here take degrees and follow the same studies all alike.

"Scholars learn first logic and rhetoric.

"So does a prisoner. With fine honeyed speech at his first coming in, he does persuade ... beseech ... that he may be lodged with one who is not itchy, to lie in a clean chamber, to lie in sheets not lousy with lice.

"But when he has no money, then he tries by subtle and cunning logic and quaint — elaborate — sophistry to make the jailkeepers trust that he will pay them later."

"Suppose they do trust him?" Sir Adam asked.

"Then he's a graduate," Sir Alexander said.

"Suppose they don't trust him?" Sir Davy Dapper asked.

Sir Alexander said, "Then he is regarded as a freshman and a sot — an idiot — and he never shall commence and get a degree, but being still barred — still prevented from graduating and still behind bars — he will be expulsed from the master's side to the twopenny ward, or else he will be placed in the hole."

The best lodgings were in the master's side, which was the most expensive, and the worst lodgings were in the hole, which was free. Money would get a prisoner better lodgings.

"I ask then when a prisoner proceeds to get an advanced degree?" Sir Adam said.

Sir Alexander said:

"When, money being the theme, he can dispute with his hard creditors' hearts and get out clear, he's then a Master of Arts."

The imprisoned debtor could try to win a debate about money with the person he owed the money to and get out of prison. The debtor could even try to persuade his creditor to forgive the debt.

A *disputatio*, or oral examination, must be passed to get an advanced degree.

Sir Alexander continued:

"Sir Davy, send your son to Wood Street College. Nowhere else can a gentleman get more knowledge."

Wood Street Counter was a debtors' prison.

"There gallants study hard," Sir Davy Dapper said.

"True, to get money," Sir Alexander said.

Sir Davy Dapper said:

"He lies by the heels, indeed."

A person who "lies by the heels" has been arrested and chained.

Sir Davy Dapper continued:

"Thanks, thanks, for your advice. I have sent for a couple of bears that shall paw him."

The bears were arresting officers.

Sergeant Curtilax and Yeoman Hanger entered the scene.

"Who comes yonder?" Sir Adam asked.

Sir Davy Dapper said, "They look like puttocks — like buzzards or arresting officers — these should be they whom I have hired to arrest my son."

"I know them," Sir Alexander said. "They are officers, sir. We'll leave you."

Sir Davy Dapper said, "My good knights, yes, leave me. You see I'm haunted now with spirits — with sergeants."

"Fare you well, sir," Sir Alexander and Sir Adam said.

They exited.

Curtilax quietly said to Hanger:

"This old muzzle-chops should be he by the fellow's description."

A person with "muzzle-chops" had a protruding jaw, resembling an animal's muzzle. Or he had a prominent nose and mouth.

The "fellow" was Sir Davy's man-servant.

Curtilax then said out loud:

"May God save you, sir."

"Come hither, you mad varlets," Sir Davy Dapper said. "Didn't my serving-man tell you I watched — I waited — here for you?"

Curtilax said, "One in a blue coat, sir, told us that in this place an old gentleman would watch for us, a thing contrary to our oath, for we are to watch for every wicked member in a city."

Servants wore blue coats.

Sir Davy Dapper said:

"You'll watch then for ten thousand."

Lots of wicked people were in the city. The officer would either try to arrest them, or if they were powerful, watch out for their interests.

He then asked:

"What's thy name, honesty?"

"Honesty" here means "good, honest fellow."

"I am named Sergeant Curtilax, sir," Curtilax answered.

Sir Davy Dapper said:

"That is an excellent name for a sergeant, Curtilax.

"Sergeants indeed are weapons of the law when prodigal ruffians are grown far in debt: Should you not cut them, citizens would be overthrown and bankrupted.

"Do thou dwell hereby in Holborn, Curtilax?"

"That's my circuit, sir," Curtilax said. "I conjure most in that circle."

When conjuring spirits, conjurors stood in a protective circle.

People joked about stands and circles: penile erections and vaginas.

Conjuring involves the raising of spirits; much sex involves the raising of penises.

"And what young, promising whelp is this?" Sir Davy Dapper asked about Hanger.

"I am of the same litter," Hanger said. "I am his yeoman — his assistant — sir; my name's Hanger."

Sir Davy Dapper said:

"Yeoman Hanger, one pair of shears surely cut out both your coats: You are two of a kind. You have two names most dangerous to men's throats. You two are villainous loads on gentlemen's backs.

"Dear ware, this Hanger and this Curtilax."

"Curtilax" means "cutlass," and swords such as cutlasses hang from a hanger on a belt.

They were on gentlemen's backs in the sense of arresting gentlemen when the gentlemen got in financial trouble.

"Dear ware" means "dear merchandise." Hangers and cutlasses could be purchased. One meaning of "dear" is expensive. Being arrested can be expensive.

Curtilax said:

"We are as other men are, sir. I cannot see but if the claws of he who makes a show of honesty and religion can fasten on what he likes, he draws blood. All who live in the world are but great fish and little fish, and feed upon one another. Some eat up whole men; a sergeant cares but for the shoulder of a man."

A usurer can figuratively eat up a whole man.

Sergeants grab men by the shoulder when arresting them. This is the heavy hand of the law.

Curtilax continued:

"They call us knaves and curs, but many times he who sets us on and has us arrest someone worries — torments — more lambs in one year than we do in seven."

Sir Davy Dapper said:

"Spoken like a noble Cerberus."

Cerberus is a guard dog in hell.

Sir Davy then asked:

"Has the action been entered?"

"His name has been entered in the book of unbelievers," Hangar said.

"What book is that?" Sir Davy Dapper asked.

"The book where all prisoners' names stand, and not one among forty when he comes in believes he will come out in haste — quickly," Curtilax said.

The Book of Unbelievers is much different from the Book of Life.

Revelation 3:5 states, "*He that overcometh, the same shall be clothed in white raiment; and I will not blot out his name out of the book of life, but I will confess his name*" (King James Version).

Some debtors spent years in prison.

Debtors' prison can be compared to hell.

"Be as dogged — as cruel — to him as your office allows you to be," Sir Davy Dapper said.

"Oh, sir!" Curtilax and Hanger said.

Sir Davy Dapper seemed to be one of those "who eat up whole men," in Curtilax' earlier words.

"Do you know the unthrift Jack Dapper?" Sir Davy Dapper asked.

An "unthrift" is a spendthrift.

"Aye, aye, sir," Curtilax said. "That gull? As well as I know my yeoman."

A gull is a fool: a gullible fool.

Sir Davy Dapper, who was incognito, asked, "And do you know his father, too: Sir Davy Dapper?"

"He is as damned a usurer as ever was among Jews," Curtilax said. "If he were sure that his father's skin would yield him any money, he would when his father dies flay it — skin it — off and sell it to cover drums for children at Bartholomew Fair."

This society was anti-Semitic, although Jews performed a valuable service as money-lenders.

Bartholomew Fair was a major festival that lasted for two weeks, beginning on Bartholomew's Day: August 24. Many items, including children's toys, were sold then.

Sir Davy Dapper said to himself:

"What toads are these to spit poison on a man to his face!"

He then said out loud:

"Do you see, my honest rascals? Yonder Greyhound is the dog he hunts with. Out of that tavern Jack Dapper will sally.

"Sa, sa; give the counter, on, set upon him."

"Greyhound" was the name of a tavern.

Jack Dapper and his man-servant, Gull, were inside the tavern.

"Sa, sa" was a hunting cry.

A counter is a prison, and to give counter is to put someone in prison.

"Give the counter" means to parry a thrust in fencing.

"Give the 'counter" means "to encounter": to go on and set upon him.

"We'll charge him upon the back, sir," Curtilax and Hanger said.

Sir Davy Dapper said, "Take no bail, put mace enough into his caudle, double your files, traverse your ground."

"Mace" is 1) an arresting sergeant's scepter or staff of office, or 2) a spice.

A "caudle" is a medicinal drink.

"Double your files" is a military term that means "put two ranks in one rank." This lengthens the file by double. Of course, Curtilax and Hanger are only two men, and so the doubled file is not very long: It is two men long. Instead of marching side by side, they could double the line by marching in single file.

"Traverse" means "move side to side."

Sir Davy Dapper was telling Curtilax and Hanger to act decisively and not spare Jack Dapper.

"We will be brave, sir," Curtilax and Hanger said.

"Cry 'arm, arm, arm,'" Sir Davy Dapper said.

In other words: Take up arms and be ready to fight.

"Thus, sir," Curtilax and Hanger said. "So we do, sir."

"There, boy! There, boy!" Sir Davy Dapper said. "Away: look to your prey, my true English wolves, and so I vanish."

"There, boy!" is a hunting cry made to a dog.

Sir Davy Dapper exited.

"Some warden of the sergeants begat this old fellow, upon my life!" Curtilax said. "Stand close."

"Shall the ambuscado — this ambush — lie in one place?" Hanger asked. "Shall we be together?"

"No, nook thou — hide thou in that nook yonder," Curtilax said.

Moll Cutpurse and Ralph Trapdoor entered the scene.

"Ralph," Moll Cutpurse said.

"What does my brave captain male and female have to say?" Ralph Trapdoor asked.

"This Holborn is such a wrangling, argumentative street," Moll Cutpurse said.

"That's because lawyers walk to and fro in it," Trapdoor said.

"Here's such jostling, as if everyone we met were drunk and reeled," Moll Cutpurse said.

"Stand, mistress," Trapdoor said. "Wait. Don't you smell carrion?"

He was talking about Curtilax and Hanger.

"Carrion" is dead flesh.

"Carrion?" Moll Cutpurse said. "No, yet I spy ravens."

She had spied Curtilax and Hanger.

Ravens feed on carrion.

"Carrion" would be the victim or victims of Curtilax and Hanger.

Trapdoor said, "Some poor wind-shaken gallant will soon fall into sore labor, and these men-midwives must bring him to bed in the counter. There all those who are great with child with debts — pregnant with debts — lie in."

High winds can do a lot of damage. Timber can be cracked by high winds; a debtor's heart can be figuratively cracked.

"Be ready to back me up," Moll Cutpurse said. "Stand up."

"Like a new maypole," Trapdoor said.

He was thinking of a penile erection.

Hanger whistled softly.

He may have been alerting Curtilax that two people — Moll Cutpurse and Trapdoor — were now present.

Curtilax made an inarticulate noise — "humph" — that indicated that he had heard Hanger's whistle and knew that the two people were present.

Seeing them, Moll Cutpurse said:

"Peeping?"

Curtilax and Hanger were watching a tavern in which Jack Dapper was drinking. When Jack Dapper came out, they planned to arrest him.

Moll Cutpurse continued:

"It shall go hard, huntsmen, but I'll spoil your game. They look for all the world like two infected maltmen coming muffled up in their cloaks during a frosty morning to London."

Maltmen came to London with malt, and they took rags back home that could be used as fertilizer. The rags were believed to be infected with the plague, and the practice was forbidden in 1630.

Jack Dapper and Gull came out of the tavern.

"A course, captain," Trapdoor said. "A bear comes to the stake."

"Course" was a hunting term meaning "a pursuit or an attack with hounds."

In bear-baiting, a bear was chained to a stake and was attacked by dogs.

Jack Dapper was the figurative bear.

"It should be so, for the dogs struggle to be let loose," Moll Cutpurse said.

The figurative dogs were the would-be arresting officers: Curtilax and Hanger. They were eager to do their job and were making appropriate noises of anticipation.

"Whew," Hanger said.

"Whew" can mean, 1) "Move quickly," or 2) "Whistle."

Hanger may have meant, "Whistle when it's time to jump quickly out of hiding and arrest Jack Dapper."

"Hemp," Curtilax said.

Hemp can be used to make hanging ropes and nooses.

As a rare verb, "to hemp" can mean "to hang" or "to halter."

If Curtilax meant "to halter," he was using it to mean to figuratively put a halter on Jack Dapper — that is, to capture him.

"Listen, Trapdoor, follow your leader," Moll Cutpurse said.

She was going to try to rescue Jack Dapper from the arresting officers, and she wanted Trapdoor to assist her.

"Gull," Jack Dapper said.

"Master," Gull said.

"Did thou ever see such an ass as I am, boy?" Jack Dapper said.

Gull said:

"No, by my truth, sir. To lose all your money, yet have false dice of your own!"

Even though Jack Dapper was cheating with loaded dice, he had lost all his money.

Gull continued:

"Why, it is as I saw a great big fellow treated the other day: He had a fair sword and buckler, and yet a butcher dry-beat him with a cudgel."

A buckler is a small shield.

"To dry-beat" means "to beat someone without drawing blood."

Moll said, "Honest sergeant —"

As she distracted the arresting officers, Trapdoor said to Jack Dapper, "Flee, flee, Master Dapper, or else you'll be arrested!"

Jack Dapper said, "Run, Gull, and draw!"

He meant: Draw your sword!

"Run, master," Gull said. "Gull follows you!"

Jack Dapper and Gull exited.

"I know you well enough," Curtilax said to Moll. "You're but a whore to hang upon any man."

Moll Cutpurse may have physically restrained him while Jack Dapper escaped, or she may have "innocently" got in Curtilax' way.

Moll replied:

"Whores then are like sergeants, so now hang you!"

Sergeants lay hands on men to arrest them; whores also lay hands on men.

Moll Cutpurse then said to Trapdoor:

"Draw, rogue, but don't strike. For a broken pate — a bleeding head — they'll keep their beds and recover twenty marks damages."

She wanted Trapdoor to draw his sword.

An injured police officer could take to his bed and exaggerate his injury in an attempt to get money for damages.

A mark is two-thirds of a pound.

Curtilax said to her:

"You shall pay for this rescue!"

He said to Hanger:

"Run down Shoe Lane and meet him."

Curtilax and Hanger exited, still hoping to arrest Jack Dapper.

As they exited, Trapdoor said after them, "Shoo! Is this a rescue, gentlemen, or not?"

He was shooing the officers to go after Jack Dapper now that Jack had a safe lead. That way, he and Moll would not be charged with a rescue. Rescuing someone — keeping someone from being arrested — was a serious offense.

Moll Cutpurse said:

"Rescue? A pox on them!

"Trapdoor, let's go away.

"I'm glad I have done perfect one good work — one good deed — today.

"If any gentleman be in scriveners' bands,

"Send but for Moll, she'll bail him by these hands."

A person in scriveners' bands has signed a contract that has put him in debt.

They exited.

CHAPTER 4

— 4.1 —

Alone in his chamber, Sir Alexander Wengrave said to himself:

"Unhappy in the follies of a son, led against judgment, sense, obedience, and all the powers of nobleness and wit.

"Oh, wretched father!"

Trapdoor entered the scene.

Sir Alexander asked him:

"Now, Trapdoor, will she come?"

Trapdoor said, "She will come in man's apparel, sir. I am in her heart — her confidence — now and share in all her secrets."

Sir Alexander and Trapdoor were going to set a trap for Moll Cutpurse. She had a reputation as a thief, and they were going to tempt her to steal by leaving some valuable items in the room where they expected her to meet Sebastian.

Sir Alexander said:

"Peace, peace, peace. Be quiet.

"Here, take my German watch; hang it up in plain sight so that I may see her hang in English — in accordance with English law — for it."

He wanted Moll to see and steal the watch. Hidden witnesses would see her do it, or it would be found in her possession later.

Stealing was a hanging offence.

"I promise you now," Trapdoor said, "that the next court sessions will rid you of her, sir. This watch will bring her in better than a hundred constables."

Sir Alexander said:

"Good Trapdoor, do thou say so? Thou cheer my heart after a storm of sorrow.

"My gold chain, too. Here, take a hundred marks in yellow links."

The yellow links were made of gold. The links were perhaps Sir Alexander's gold chain of office as magistrate, but in this society, well-dressed gentlemen wore gold necklaces.

Sir Alexander wanted Moll to steal the gold chain, too.

"That will do well to bring the watch to light, sir," Trapdoor said, "and it is worth a thousand of your headboroughs' lanterns."

"Links" can be lit torches that provide light.

A night watch is a group of constables who watch out for the safety of citizens during the night.

A headborough is a parish constable.

"Place that in the court cupboard," Sir Alexander said. "Let it lie full in the view of her thief-whorish eye."

A court cupboard had three display shelves.

"She cannot miss it, sir," Trapdoor said. "I see it so plainly that I could steal it myself."

"Perhaps thou shall, too," Sir Alexander said. "That or something as weighty; what she leaves, thou shall come secretly in and filch away, and all the weight upon her back I'll lay."

"You cannot assure that, sir," Trapdoor said.

"No? What prevents me from doing it?" Sir Alexander said.

"Being a stout — a robust — girl," Trapdoor said, "perhaps she'll desire pressing, then all the weight must lie upon her belly."

One punishment used to make someone confess was to load heavy weights until the person either confessed or was pressed to death.

Moll Cutpurse might prefer pressing to confessing.

Trapdoor meant that all the weight must lie upon her belly when she is in the missionary position.

"Belly or back, I don't care so long as I've won," Sir Alexander said.

Interpreting "won" as "one," Trapdoor said, "You're of my mind for that, sir."

He wanted to sexually have Moll Cutpurse either in the front or in the back.

"Hang up my ruff band and hang a diamond with it," Sir Alexander said. "It may be she'll like that best."

A ruff band is a ruff collar.

Trapdoor said to himself:

"It's well for her that she must have her choice; he thinks nothing too good for her."

Sir Alexander was tempting Moll to steal a multitude of valuable objects.

Trapdoor then said out loud:

"If you hold on this mind a little longer, to turn thief myself shall be the first work I do; it would do a man good to be hanged when he is so well provided for."

According to the *Oxford English Dictionary*, an obsolete meaning of "hanged" is "To remain or rely in faith or expectation; to count or depend confidently *on*." With such valuable items in his possession, a man could be hanged: confident that he could provide for himself.

The valuables that Sir Alexander was tempting Moll Cutpurse to steal were so valuable that Trapdoor was tempted to steal them first.

Sir Alexander said:

"So, well done; all hangs well, and I wish that she hung so, too. The sight of her hanging would please me more than all their glistenings.

"Oh, that my mysteries — the knowledge that I as a father have acquired — to such straits should run that I must rob myself to bless and protect my son!"

Sir Alexander and Trapdoor exited.

Sebastian entered the scene. With him was Mary Fitzallard, who was dressed like a page (a boy-servant), and Moll, who was dressed in men's clothing.

"Thou have done me a kind office — a kind service — without touch either of sin or shame," Sebastian said to Moll. "Our loves are honest."

He meant the loves of Mary Fitzallard and himself.

"I'd scorn to make such shift to bring you together else," Moll Cutpurse said.

"Shift" can mean 1) effort, or 2) change of clothes.

Moll Cutpurse was responsible for Mary Fitzallard dressing as a page.

"Now I have time and opportunity without all fear to bid thee welcome, love," Sebastian said to Mary Fitzallard.

They kissed.

"Never with more desire and harder venture," Mary Fitzallard said.

Moll Cutpurse said to them, "How strange this looks: one man to kiss another."

"I'd choose to kiss such men, Moll," Sebastian said. "I think a woman's lip tastes well in a doublet."

A doublet is a jacket for a man. Any women who wore them would probably be rebels or outcasts in one way or another. Moll herself is a rebel against her society's constraints for women.

"Many an old madam has the better fortune then, whose breaths grew stale before the fashion came," Moll Cutpurse said. "If men's clothes will help them, as you think it will do, they'll learn in time to pluck on the hose, too —"

Moll was joking that since kissing a woman dressed in men's clothing was fashionable (at least to Sebastian), many old women would start dressing in men's jackets and even in men's hose so that they would be kissed.

Sebastian said:

"— the older they — the old madams — grow."

He may have meant that the older the old women grow, the more masculine clothing they would learn to put on.

Sebastian continued:

"In truth, I speak seriously — as some have a conceit or fancy that their drink tastes better in an outlandish cup than in our own, so I think that every kiss she gives me now in this strange form is worth a pair of two."

Kissing a woman dressed in men's clothing was a turn-on for Sebastian. This was his fetish: He enjoyed kissing a cross-dressing woman.

Sebastian continued:

"Here we are safe and furthest from the eye of all suspicion. This is my father's chamber, upon which floor he never steps until night.

"Here he does not mistrust or suspect me, nor do I suspect his coming.

"At my own chamber he still spies on me. My freedom is not there — I can't find it there, where I am checked and curbed. Here he shall miss his purpose."

Moll Cutpurse said:

"And what's your business now that you have what you wanted, sir?

"At your great suit — your earnest request — I promised you that I would come here. I pitied her for name's sake."

"Moll" was a nickname for "Mary." Traditionally, "Moll" was also a nickname for a "low" woman.

Moll Cutpurse continued:

"That a Moll should be so crossed in love when there's so many who own nine lays apiece, and not so little."

In other words: Many women named Moll have nine places where they can have sex — and not so little a number as nine.

These Molls were probably prostitutes.

Moll Cutpurse concluded:

"My tailor outfitted her. How do you like his work?"

"So well that no art can improve it for this purpose," Sebastian said, "but to thy wit and help we're chiefly in debt and must live always beholden to you."

"Any honest pity I'm willing to bestow upon poor ring-doves," Moll Cutpurse said.

"Ring-doves" are literally wood-doves and figuratively lovebirds or lovers.

"I'll offer no worse play," Sebastian said.

In other words: I won't try to have sex with Mary Fitzallard right now.

"Play" can be 1) entertainment in general, or 2) sexual play in particular.

"Nay, and if you should, sir, I would draw first and prove the quicker man," Moll Cutpurse said.

She would draw her sword and defend Mary Fitzallard.

But the drawing of a weapon can have a sexual meaning: The "weapon" can be a penis. So perhaps Moll would be quicker than Sebastian and have sex with Mary first.

Sebastian said:

"Hold, there shall need no weapon at this meeting; but so that thou shall not loose thy fury in vain —"

Hanging on the wall was a viol de gamba, which is similar to a modern violoncello, aka cello. It was a large string instrument that was played between the musician's legs, giving rise to sexual humor.

Taking the musical instrument from the wall, Sebastian handed it to Moll and continued:

"— here, take this viol, run upon the guts, and end thy quarrel singing."

Poetic fury is poetic inspiration. "Poetic" includes "musical."

"Run upon the guts" can mean 1) draw a bow across the guts (strings) of the viol, 2) stick a sword through someone's guts, or 3) stick a 'sword' through someone's guts.

Moll Cutpurse said:

"Like a swan above a bridge."

Some people believed swans sang before they die.

She continued:

"Look, here's the bridge, and here I am above it."

A bridge is a piece of wood over which the strings of a string instrument are stretched.

"Go on, sweet Moll, and sing," Sebastian requested.

"I've heard her much commended, sir, for one who was never taught," Mary Fitzallard said.

"I'm much beholden to them," Moll Cutpurse said. "Well, since you'll necessarily put us together, sir, I'll play my part as well as I can; it shall never be said I came into a gentleman's chamber and took his instrument down by the walls."

Moll had never entered a gentleman's chamber and taken his musical instrument down from where it hung on the walls.

In addition, she had never been by the walls of a gentleman's chamber and taken down his "instrument" — she had never made the gentleman's erect penis not erect.

Moll's playing her part as well as she could meant 1) playing the viol, and/or 2) masturbating.

"Why, well done, Moll!" Sebastian said. "Indeed, it had been a shame for that gentleman then who would have let it hung still and never offered it to thee."

Moll Cutpurse said, "There it should have been still then as far as I, Moll, am concerned, for although the world judges impudently of me, I never came into that chamber yet where I took down the instrument myself."

Sebastian said, "Bah, let them prate abroad — let them all talk and gossip around the town; thou are here where thou are known and loved. There are a thousand secretive dames who will call the viol an unmannerly instrument for a woman and therefore talk broadly and crudely of thee, when you shall have them sit wider to a worse quality."

Some women who criticized Moll for playing the viol with her legs apart themselves parted their own legs wider for a male organic instrument.

"Bah," Moll said. "I always fall asleep and don't think about them, sir, and thus I dream."

Sebastian said, "Please, let's hear thy dream — thy song — Moll."

"Dream" can mean "sing and play a musical instrument."

Moll Cutpurse sang:

"*I dream there is a mistress,*

"*And she lays out the money;*

"*She goes unto her sisters.*"

The "sisters" may be friends.

Moll continued singing:

"*She never comes at any.*"

In other words: She never sexually accosts anyone.

Sir Alexander entered the scene, and he watched and listened from a hiding place, unseen.

Moll continued singing:

"*She says she went to the Burse for patterns.*

"*You shall find her at Saint Kathern's,*

"*And comes home with never a penny.*"

The Burse is the Royal Exchange, which had many shops, including shops for silks and draperies.

Saint Kathern's is the dockside district of London's East End. It had many taverns and a bad reputation.

"That's a free mistress, indeed," Sebastian said.

The adjective "free" can mean 1) generous, or 2) loose and wanton.

In the song, the woman — a wife — goes out with friends, perhaps to drink, and she spends all her money after telling her husband that she is going shopping.

The woman in Moll's first song may give the appearance of wrong-doing, yet she enjoys freedom and does not engage in unethical sex.

Sir Alexander said to himself, "Aye, aye, aye, like her who sings it, one of thine own choosing."

"But shall I dream — sing — again?" Moll asked.

She sang:

"*Here comes a wench [who] will brave [defy] ye,*

"*Her courage was so great:*

"*She lay with one of the navy,*

"*Her husband lying in the Fleet,*"

Fleet was the name of a prison.

Moll continued singing:

"Yet oft with him she cavilled [quarreled].

"I wonder what she ails [what ails her].

"Her husband's ship lay gravelled,"

"Gravelled" can mean "stranded" or "beached."

Her husband's penis was also out of commission.

Moll continued singing:

"When hers could hoise up sails."

The "sails" are skirts.

The woman's husband was in prison, and so he could not move around freely, but the woman could move around freely.

Prostitutes have many clients, and neighbors will notice a constant stream of visitors. One way to maintain her reputation for a while is for the prostitute to say that she is the wife of a ship captain and that the visitors are sailors bringing her news about her husband and his ship. For example, she could pretend that a visitor had told her that he had seen her husband's ship in such-and-such a port.

Moll continued singing:

"Yet she began like all my foes

"To call 'whore' first, for so do those:

"A pox of [on] all false tails!"

"Tails" is 1) a pun on "tales," and 2) sex organs.

"False" can mean "adulterous" and "unchaste."

In Moll's second song, a woman whose husband was in prison had an affair with a sailor, yet she called Moll a whore.

The woman had engaged in unethical sex, yet she falsely accused Moll of engaging in unethical sex.

"By the Virgin Mary, amen, say I," Sebastian said.

"So say I, too," Sir Alexander said to himself.

Moll said:

"Hang up the viol now, sir.

"All this while I was in a dream; one shall lie rudely then, but being awake, I keep my legs together."

Seeing the German watch, she said:

"A watch. What's the time here?"

"Now, now, she's trapped," Sir Alexander said to himself.

He thought that she would steal the German watch he had left out for her to steal.

Moll Cutpurse said:

"Between one and two; nay, then I don't care.

"A watch and a musician are cousin-germans — first cousins — in one thing: They must both keep time well, or there's no goodness in them; the one else deserves to be dashed against a wall, and the other to have his brains knocked out with a fiddle case.

"What? A loose chain and a dangling diamond.

"Here would be a brave booty for an evening-thief now. There's many a younger brother who would be glad to look twice in at a window for it, and wriggle in and out, like an eel in a sandbag."

Younger brothers inherit little or nothing and so would be glad to get into possession of more money.

An eel in a sandbag is in a place where it ought not to be.

Moll continued:

"Oh, if men's secret youthful faults should judge them, it would be the most general — involving almost everyone — execution that ever was seen in England.

"There would be but few left to sing the ballads about the condemned.

"There would be so much work. Most of our brokers would be chosen for hangmen: a good day for them. They might renew their wardrobes free of cost then."

Brokers can be dealers in secondhand clothing.

In this society, hangmen were awarded the clothing of those whom they executed.

"This is the roaring wench who must do us good," Sebastian said.

"No poison, sir, but serves us for some use, which is confirmed in her," Mary Fitzallard said.

Moll Cutpurse was supposed to be a bad woman, but she could do good, too. She was currently helping Sebastian and Mary.

Sir Alexander sighed. His plan was not working: Moll was not stealing any valuables.

"Peace! Quiet!" Sebastian said. "By God's foot, I did hear him surely, wherever he is!"

"Who did you hear?" Moll asked.

"My father," Sebastian said. "It was like a sigh of his; I must be wary."

Sir Alexander said to himself:

"No, this plot will not be successful. Am I alone so wretched that nothing takes?"

Sir Alexander continued saying to himself:

"I'll put him to his plunge for it."

"Plunge" means "straits" or "dilemma." Sir Alexander would put Sebastian in a difficult position; he would be over his head in troubles.

Sir Alexander stepped into the open.

Seeing his father, Sebastian said:

"By God's life, here he comes!"

He gave Moll some money and said for the benefit of his father:

"Sir, I beseech you take it as payment for your viol lesson. Your way of teaching does so much content me, I'll make it four pounds. Here's forty shillings, sir."

A pound was twenty shillings, so he was offering her two pounds: half of the actual fee of four pounds.

Sebastian continued:

"I think I name it right."

He whispered to Moll:

"Help me, good Moll."

He then said out loud:

"Forty in hand."

He was pretending that Moll, who was dressed in men's clothing, was a man and a music teacher. He did not know that Sir Alexander knew very well who she was.

Moll Cutpurse said, "Sir, you shall pardon me. I have more from the meanest scholar I can teach. This meanest scholar pays me more than you have offered yet."

"At the next quarter when I receive the means my father allows me, you shall have the other forty shillings," Sebastian said.

Sir Alexander said to himself:

"This would be well now, were it to a man whose sorrows had blind eyes, but my sorrows behold his follies and untruths with two clear glasses."

He then walked over to the others and asked out loud:

"How are things now? What is going on?"

"Sir," Sebastian said.

"Who is he there?" Sir Alexander said, pretending not to know who Moll was.

"You're come in good time, sir," Sebastian said. "I've a suit — an earnest request — to make to you. I'd crave your present kindness."

"Who is he there?" Sir Alexander asked again.

"A gentleman, a musician, sir, one of excellent fingering," Sebastian said.

Sir Alexander said to himself, "Aye, I think so; I wonder how they escaped her notice."

Moll was supposed to be a thief: one with excellent fingering when it came to picking up items that did not belong to her. Sir Alexander wondered why she had not stolen the valuable items that had been laid out to trap her.

"Fingering" also has a bawdy meaning.

"He has the most delicate stroke, sir," Sebastian said.

The stroke can be sexual in nature. Or it can be musical. Or medical.

"A stroke indeed," Sir Alexander said to himself. "I feel it at my heart."

"He puts down all your famous musicians," Sebastian said.

"Puts down" means 1) surpasses them in music, 2) kills them by giving them a venereal disease, or 3) makes their penile erections go down in bed.

"Aye, a whore may put down a hundred of them," Sir Alexander said to himself.

"Them" can mean "penises."

"Forty shillings is the agreement, sir, between us," Sebastian said. "Now, sir, my present means amounts only to half of it."

"Forty shillings" is the amount that Sebastian wanted to pay as a partial payment, although Moll had NOT agreed to it. Forty shillings, aka two pounds, was half of the four pounds they had agreed to be the full payment.

"And he stands upon the whole," Sir Alexander said. "He wants the whole payment now."

"Mounts," "stands," and "whole" [hole] all have bawdy meanings.

"Aye, indeed he does, sir," Sebastian said.

"And will do still," Sir Alexander said to himself. "He'll never be in other tale."

In other words: 1) The musician will never be given full payment; people will always be owing him, 2) The musician will always insist that four pounds is the amount owed, and 3) The musician will never change his story — he will always insist to Sir Alexander that he is a musician.

"He'll never be in other tale" can mean 1) He'll never tell a different story, or 2) He'll never forget the debt, or 3) He'll never be in other "tail" — in someone else's vagina.

Of course, Sir Alexander knew that the musician was Moll Cutpurse.

"Therefore, I'd stop his mouth, sir, if I could," Sebastian said.

Sir Alexander replied:

"Hmm, true, there is no other way indeed."

He then said to himself:

"His folly hardens; shame must necessarily follow."

He then said out loud to Moll:

"Now, sir, I understand you profess music: You claim to be skilled in music."

"I am a poor servant to that liberal science, sir," Moll Cutpurse said.

"Where is it you teach?" Sir Alexander asked.

"Right next to Clifford's Inn," Moll Cutpurse said.

"Hmm, that's a fit place for it," Sir Alexander said. "Do you have many scholars?"

"And some of worth whom I may call my masters," Moll Cutpurse said.

Sir Alexander said to himself:

"Aye, true, a company of whoremasters."

"Whoremasters" are the clients of whores.

Sir Alexander said out loud:

"You teach to sing, too?"

This kind of singing may be making sounds during sex.

"By the Virgin Mary, I do, sir," Moll Cutpurse said.

"I think you'll find an apt scholar of my son, especially for prick-song," Sir Alexander said.

"Prick-song" is music that is pricked down — that is, it is written down.

"I have much hope of him," Moll Cutpurse said.

Sir Alexander said to himself:

"I am sorry for it; I have the less hope for him because of that."

He then said out loud:

"You can play any lesson?"

"Lessons" are musical compositions used in teaching music.

"At first sight, sir," Moll Cutpurse said.

"There's a thing called 'The Witch,'" Sir Alexander said. "Can you play that?"

"I would be sorry anyone should mend me — be able to help me to improve — in it," Moll Cutpurse said.

Sir Alexander said to himself:

"Aye, I believe thee. Thou have so bewitched my son that no care will mend the work that thou have done.

"I have thought myself, since my art fails, that I'll make her policy — her stratagem of posing as a musician — the art to trap her."

His plot to tempt Moll to be a thief had failed, so he needed another plot to get her hung.

Sir Alexander continued saying to himself:

"Here are four angels marked with holes in them, fit for his — Sebastian's — cracked companions; he will give her gold. These cracked angels I will make induction — the first step — to her ruin and rid shame from my house and grief from my heart."

Coins were made of gold and silver, and people would clip off bits of the precious metal. Coins had a ring around the depiction of a king's or queen's head. If that ring was damaged, the coin was "cracked" and no longer legal tender.

"Cracked companions" means "immoral companions."

Moll's vulva has a crack.

The holes drilled in the angels — gold coins — could be used for purposes of identification. Sir Alexander may have been intending to have Moll arrested later for stealing them, but such damaged coins were no longer legal tender, and Moll could get in legal trouble for possessing them.

Sir Alexander said out loud:

"Here, son, in what you take content and pleasure, want shall not curb you."

Sir Alexander gave him the cracked angels and said, "Pay in gold the gentleman his latter half of payment owed to him."

"I thank you, sir," Sebastian said.

"Oh, may the operation of it end three: life in her, shame in him, and grief in me," Sir Alexander said to himself.

Sir Alexander hoped that the plot would end Moll's life, Sebastian's shame (in loving Moll), and his own grief (that Sebastian loved Moll).

Sir Alexander exited.

"Indeed, thou shall have them," Sebastian said to Moll. "It is my father's gift. Never was man beguiled with better shift."

"He who can mistake me for a male musician, I cannot choose but make him my instrument and play upon him," Moll Cutpurse said.

Everyone exited.

Mistress Gallipot and Mistress Openwork talked together in Openwork's house. Goshawk was pursuing Mistress Openwork, and Laxton was pursuing Mistress Gallipot.

"Is then that bird of yours, Master Goshawk, so wild?" Mistress Gallipot asked.

"A goshawk, a puttock: all for prey. He angles for fish, but he loves flesh better," Mistress Openwork said.

A "puttock" is the bird called a kite.

"Fish" can figuratively mean "women."

"Is it possible that his smooth face should have wrinkles in it and we not see them?" Mistress Gallipot asked.

In other words: Is it possible that his handsome face is hiding villainy?

"Possible!" Mistress Openwork said. "Why, don't many handsome legs in silk stockings have villainous splay feet despite all their great roses?"

Gallants wore silk stockings.

"Splay feet" are feet that turn outward.

"Roses" made of silk were decorations worn on the shoes.

"Indeed, sirrah, thou say the truth," Mistress Gallipot said.

"Didn't thou ever see an archer as thou have walked by Bunhill Street look a-squint — out of the corners of his eyes — when he drew his bow?" Mistress Openwork asked.

"Yes, when his arrows have flown toward Islington suburb, his eyes have shot clean contrary towards Pimlico Tavern," Mistress Gallipot said.

In other words: The arrow went in one direction while the archer's eyes looked in another direction.

"For all the world so does Master Goshawk double — be duplicitous — with me," Mistress Openwork said.

Goshawk was trying to do two things: 1) He was trying to convince Mistress Openwork that her husband is unfaithful to her, and 2) He was trying to get her in bed.

"Oh, fie upon him!" Mistress Gallipot said. "If he doubles once, he's not for me."

"Because Goshawk goes in a shag-ruff band, with a face sticking up in it that looks like an agate set in a cramp-ring, he thinks I'm in love with him," Mistress Openwork said.

Goshawk thought that being dressed as a gallant attracted women.

A cramp-ring was a ring that was supposed to ward off cramp. Some people today believe that copper bracelets can ward off the pain of arthritis.

Goshawk's sense of fashion, however, was faulty. His ruff was too big, and it made his head look too small.

"Alas, I think he takes his mark amiss in thee," Mistress Gallipot said.

"He has by often beating into me — repeatedly telling me — made me believe that my husband kept a whore," Mistress Openwork said.

"Very 'good,'" Mistress Gallipot said sarcastically.

"He swore to me that my husband this very morning went in a boat with a tilt — an awning — over it to the Three Pigeons Inn at Brainford, and his punk — his whore — was with him under his tilt," Mistress Openwork said.

A penis can suddenly tilt upward.

"That would be 'wholesome,'" Mistress Gallipot said sarcastically.

Cough. Hole. Cough.

"I believed it; I fell a-swearing at my husband and cursing of harlots," Mistress Openwork said. "His story made me ready to hoise up sail, and be there as soon as he."

"Hoise up sail" can mean "lift a skirt."

"So, so," Mistress Gallipot said.

"And for that voyage Goshawk comes hither incontinently: with an excessive sexual appetite," Mistress Openwork said. "But, sirrah, this water-spaniel dives after no duck but me; his hope is sexually having me at Brainford to make me cry quack."

Mistress Openwork was the "duck" whom Goshawk is pursuing, and he wanted her to "quack" loudly during orgasm.

"Are thou sure of it?" Mistress Gallipot asked.

Mistress Openwork said:

"Sure of it! My poor innocent Openwork came in as I was poking my ruff: using a poking stick to set the plaits of my ruff."

A "ruff" can also be a candle, so one meaning of "poking my ruff" is "masturbating with a candle."

Mistress Openwork continued:

"Immediately I hit him in the teeth — I reproached him — with the Three Pigeons Inn. He denied all, I up and told him all, and now he stands in a nearby shop like a musket on a rest, to hit Goshawk in the eye when he comes to fetch me to the boat."

The rest is a support for the musket. The end of the musket lies on the rest, while the marksman aims and fires.

Mistress Gallipot said, "Such another lame gelding offered to carry me through thick and thin — Laxton, sirrah — but I am rid of him now."

"Happy is the woman who can be rid of them all," Mistress Openwork said. "Alas, what are your whisking — brisk and lively — gallants compared to our husbands, weigh them rightly man for man?"

"Indeed, mere shallow things," Mistress Gallipot said.

"Shallow things" may mean "short penises."

Mistress Openwork said:

"Idle, foolish, useless, simple things, running — flighty — heads, and yet let them run over us never so fast, when all's done, we shopkeepers are sure to have them in our purse-nets at length, and when they are in, Lord, what simple animals they are!"

"Running heads" may also mean "diseased penises."

"Purse-nets" are bag-shaped nets used to catch small animals such as rabbits.

The "purse-nets" are also traps for catching the whisking gallants.

The shopkeepers set traps — enticements — to catch shoppers' money in the shopkeepers' purse-nets.

"Purse-nets" may also be vaginas.

Mistress Openwork continued:

"And after they are caught in the purse-net, then they hang the head."

"Then they droop," Mistress Gallipot said.

"Hang the head" and "droop" have bawdy meanings. Penises do this after ejaculation.

Possibly, the gallants are financially embarrassed and are in debt to the shopkeepers and so they try to get on the shopkeepers' wives' good side so the wives will plead with their husbands to be lenient to the gallants.

"Then they write letters," Mistress Openwork said.

"Then they cog," Mistress Gallipot said.

"Cog" means 1) cheat, and 2) wheedle, perhaps by using fake flattery.

Mistress Openwork said, "Then they deal underhand with us, and we must ingle with our husbands a-bed, and we must swear they are our cousins and are able to do us a pleasure at court."

"Ingle" means 1) caress, or 2) cajole.

An "ingle" can be a boy kept for homosexual purposes, so perhaps when the wives ingle with their husbands, the wives do what male homosexuals do: oral and/or anal sex.

The "pleasure at court" could be a political favor, or a sexual orgasm.

Mistress Gallipot said:

"And yet when we have done our best, all's but put into a riven — a broken — dish: we are only frumped at — mocked and insulted — and libeled upon."

A "riven dish" may be a vulva. Vulvas are cracked.

Mistress Gallipot continued:

"Oh, if it were the good Lord's will, there would be a law made that decrees that no citizen should trust any of them at all!" Mistress Openwork said.

Having affairs with gallants has its downsides. The gallants may be bad in bed, may not keep the affair secret, and may cause trouble with a husband whom the wife must soothe.

Goshawk entered the scene. He was meeting Mistress Openwork, and he did not expect to see Mistress Gallipot. He had told Mistress Openwork that he would take her to a place where she could see her husband having an affair, but he was hoping to start an affair with her.

Mistress Gallipot whispered to Mistress Openwork, "Hush, sirrah. Goshawk flutters."

"How are things now?" Goshawk asked Mistress Openwork. "Are you ready?"

"Nay, are you ready?" Mistress Openwork said. "A little thing, you see, makes us ready."

Hmm. "A little thing ... makes us ready"? Even a little penis makes these two women ready to have sex?

Mistress Openwork may have meant that they were almost ready, with only a little left to do.

"Us?" Goshawk asked. "Why, must she make one — join us — in the voyage?"

"Oh, by any means," Mistress Openwork said. "Do I know how my husband will handle and treat me?"

She was pretending that she wanted Mistress Gallipot with her as support when she confronted her husband: Openwork.

Goshawk said to himself:

"By God's foot, how shall I find water to keep these two mills going?"

In this society, one meaning of "water" is "semen." He was wondering how he could sexually satisfy both wives.

Goshawk then said to himself:

"Well, since you'll necessarily be clapped under hatches, if I don't sail with you both until all split, hang me up at the mainyard and dunk me."

"Clapped under hatches" means "kept below deck," but "clapped" also means "embraced."

"To make all split" means "to wreak havoc" or "to be shipwrecked."

"All split" can refer to a ship's hull, or to a woman's legs and pudenda.

Goshawk was going to do his best to sexually satisfy both wives.

Goshawk then said to himself:

"It's but liquoring them both soundly and getting them drunk, and then you shall see their cork heels fly up high, like two swans when their tails are above water and their long necks under water, diving to catch gudgeons."

Some fashionable shoes had cork heels.

Women with light heels have heels that are easily and quickly lifted in the air for sex in the missionary position.

Gudgeons are small fish that are easily caught, and so "gudgeon" came to be a slang word for "fool."

Goshawk didn't know it, but these two women were out to catch a gudgeon: Goshawk.

Goshawk said out loud:

"Come, come, oars stand ready, the tide's with us: on with those false faces: those masks. Blow, winds, and thou shall take thy husband casting out his net to catch fresh salmon at Brainford."

"Fresh salmon" is "young whores."

"I believe you'll eat of a cod's head of your own dressing before you reach halfway thither," Mistress Gallipot said.

Goshawk was figuratively preparing a cod's head so it could be eaten, and Mistress Gallipot said he would eat it. He would reap the reward of his effort.

But a "cod's head" is also slang for a "fool," and Mistress Gallipot also meant that he would catch himself in his own net.

"Eat of a cod's head" may have a bawdy meaning. A codpiece was a pouch worn over a man's genitals.

Mistress Gallipot's words may mean that Goshawk would "eat" his own semen. This need not be meant literally.

Certainly, Goshawk was preparing semen, but Mistress Gallipot did not think that it would go where Goshawk wanted it to go. Rather, it would stay in Goshawk's body.

Sperm cells that are not released will eventually die and be reabsorbed back into the man's body.

"So, so, follow close," Goshawk said. "Pin your masks as you go."

The women donned masks.

Laxton entered the scene. His face was partially covered.

"Do you hear me?" Laxton said to Mistress Gallipot.

"Yes, I thank my ears," she replied.

"I must have a bout with your apothecaryship," Laxton said.

"Bout" can mean "sexual encounter," although Laxton had avoided having sex with Mistress Gallipot.

"Bout" can also refer to fighting.

"At what weapon?" Mistress Gallipot said.

One "weapon" is between a man's legs.

"I must speak with you," Laxton said.

"No," Mistress Gallipot said.

"No?" Laxton said. "You shall."

"Shall?" Mistress Gallipot said. "Go away, you soused sturgeon — half fish, half flesh!"

"Soused sturgeon" is pickled sturgeon.

"Half fish, half flesh" is neither one nor the other. Laxton's sexuality is in question. Does he have stones, aka testicles? Does he use them? Is he impotent?

"Indeed, gib, are you spitting?" Laxton said. "I'll cut your tail, pusscat, for this."

"Gib" means "cat." It, like "pussycat," is meant to be an insult.

Mistress Gallipot said:

"Alas, poor Laxton, I think thy tail's cut already."

Laxton's "tail" is between his legs.

She continued:

"So do your worst!"

Laxton said, "If I do not —"

He exited.

Goshawk said:

"Come, have you finished?"

Master Openwork entered the scene.

Goshawk whispered to Mistress Rosamond Openwork:

"By God's foot, Rosamond, your husband!"

Openwork said:

"How are things now? Sweet Master Goshawk, none is more welcome than you.

"I have wanted — lacked — your embracements and missed your company. When friends meet, the music of the spheres does not sound more sweeter than does their conference: their conversation."

In Ptolemaic astronomy, crystalline spheres containing the sun, planets, and stars revolved around the Earth. As they moved, they created music.

Just a few minutes earlier, Mistress Openwork had said about her husband that "now he stands in a nearby shop like a musket on a rest, to hit Goshawk in the eye when he comes to fetch me to the boat."

Possibly, Mistress Openwork and her husband had reconciled and would now carry out a plan to torment Goshawk.

Openwork then said:

"Who is this? Rosamond? My wife?"

He asked Mistress Gallipot:

"How are things now, sister?"

Goshawk whispered to Mistress Openwork, "Silence, if you love me."

"Why masked?" Overwork asked.

"Does a mask grieve you, sir?" Mistress Openwork asked.

"It does," Openwork said.

"Then you had best get you a-mumming," Mistress Openwork said.

To be mum is to be quiet.

Mummers' plays were mimed; they had no dialogue.

Goshawk whispered to Mistress Openwork, "By God's foot, you'll spoil all!"

Mistress Gallipot asked, "Mayn't we cover our bare faces with masks as well as you cover your bald heads with hats?"

Openwork said:

"No masks.

"Why, they are thieves to beauty; they rob eyes of admiration in which true love lies.

"Why are masks worn? Why are they good, or why are they desired, unless by their gay covers wits are fired to read the vilest looks?"

Beautiful masks make men look at ugly, masked women.

Openwork continued:

"Many bad faces, because rich gems are treasured up in jewel-cases, pass by their privilege current, but as caves damn misers' gold, so masks are beauty's graves."

Many people think that under a mask is a beautiful face, but sometimes, the face is not beautiful.

A beautiful face under a face is like misers' gold hidden in a cave. Beautiful faces should be seen and enjoyed, and misers' gold should be spent and enjoyed.

Openwork continued:

"Men never meet women with such muffled eyes but they curse her who first did devise masks, and they swear it was some beldam: some witch or hag.

"Come, take your mask off."

"I will not," Mistress Openwork said.

Openwork said:

"Good faces masked are jewels kept by sprites [by spirits].

"Hide none but bad ones, for they poison men's sights.

"Show them as shopkeepers do their braided stuff,

"By owl-light; fine wares cannot be open enough."

"Stuff" is fabric.

"Braided stuff" is goods whose colors have faded. Shopkeepers could keep the light low in their shops so shoppers would not know that the colors had faded.

Fine merchandise can be displayed in bright light.

Openwork continued:

"Please, sweet Rose, come strike this sail. Take off your mask."

"Sail?" Mistress Rosamond Openwork said.

"Huh?" Openwork said. "Yes, wife, strike sail, for storms are in thine eyes."

"They are here, sir, in my brows if any rise," Mistress Openwork said.

If she becomes angry, she will frown.

Openwork said:

"Huh, brows?"

He then said to Mistress Gallipot:

"What does she say, friend? Please tell me why your two flags were advanced."

In theaters, flags were raised to announce performances.

Here, the "flags" are masks.

Openwork continued:

"The comedy, come. Tell me, what's the comedy?"

Mistress Gallipot said, "*Westward Ho!*"

Thomas Dekker and John Webster co-wrote a comedy titled *Westward Ho!* In the comedy, citizens' wives and gallants sailed west to Brainford. The gallants wanted to seduce the citizens' wives but were unsuccessful.

Rivermen on the Thames announced they were rowing west with the cry "Westward Ho!"

Goshawk, Mistress Openwork, and Mistress Gallipot were supposed to sail west to Brainford.

"What?" Openwork asked.

"It is *Westward Ho*, she says," Mistress Openwork said.

"Are you both mad?" Goshawk asked.

Mistress Openwork said to her husband, "Is it market day at Brainford, and your ware — your merchandise — not sent up yet?"

Goshawk had told her that her husband was meeting a whore there.

"What market day?" Openwork said. "What ware?"

"A pie with three pigeons in it," Mistress Openwork said. "It is drawn from the oven and awaits your cutting up."

She was referring to the Three Pigeons Inn.

A "pigeon" may mean a "wild fowl" — a prostitute.

"Cutting up" can mean "having sex."

Goshawk whispered to Mistress Openwork, "As you regard my credit and reputation —"

She was tormenting him.

"Are thou mad?" Openwork asked his wife.

"Yes, lecherous goat, baboon!" Mistress Openwork said.

Goats and baboons had reputations as lascivious animals.

"Baboon?" Openwork said. "Then toss me in a blanket."

Being tossed in a blanket was a punishment.

"Do I do it well?" Mistress Openwork asked Mistress Gallipot.

She was tormenting both Goshawk and her husband.

"Rarely," Mistress Gallipot said. "Splendidly."

"Likely, sir, she's not well," Goshawk said. "It's best to leave her."

A husband should leave an ill wife? What about "in sickness and in health"?

"No, I'll stand and withstand the storm now no matter how fierce it blows," Openwork said.

"Did I for this lose all my friends?" Mistress Openwork asked. "Did I for this refuse rich hopes and golden fortunes just to be made a stale to a common whore?"

A "stale" is a laughingstock. Here, the stale is a former lover who is laughed at by the lover who has replaced her.

"This amazes me!" Openwork said.

"Oh, God! Oh, God! Do thou feed at reversion now? Do thou feed at a strumpet's leaving?" Mistress Openwork said.

"Reversion" can mean 1) leftover food, or 2) legal right of succession after death or the expiration of a grant.

In other words: She was asking if something had happened to her husband's whore and if he was willing to come back to her, his wife?

Astonished, Openwork said, "Rosamond —"

Goshawk said to himself, "I sweat! I wish I lay in Cold Harbor!"

If he were cold, he would stop sweating. Also, if he were in Cold Harbor, he would not be here and would not be tormented by Mistress Openwork.

"Thou have struck ten thousand daggers through my heart!" Mistress Openwork said.

"Not I, by heaven, sweet wife," Openwork said.

"Go, devil, go," Mistress Openwork said. "That which thou swear by damns thee."

In other words: You swear by Heaven, but Heaven damns you.

Goshawk whispered to her, "By God's heart, will you undo and ruin me?"

"Why do you stay here?" Mistress Openwork said to her husband. "The star — the whore — by which you sail shines yonder above Chelsea; you lose your shore — your destination — if you stay here. If this moon lights you, seek out your light whore."

Moonlight is low light; a light whore is wanton.

"Huh?" Openwork said.

"Bah!" Mistress Openwork said. "Your western pug —"

"Western pugs" navigated barges westward.

A "pug" can also be a whore.

Goshawk said to himself, "By God's wounds, now hell roars!"

Mistress Openwork continued, "— with whom you tilted in a pair of oars this very morning."

"Tilted" can mean 1) jousted, including sexual "jousting," or 2) pitched on the waves in a boat. "Pitching" can occur during lovemaking.

"A pair of oars" can mean a boat.

"Oars?" Openwork asked.

"At Brainford, sir," Mistress Openwork said.

Openwork replied:

"Rack not my patience."

The rack was a medieval instrument of torture.

He then said:

"Master Goshawk, some slave has buzzed — whispered — this into her ear, hasn't he?

"Did I run atilt — engage in a sexual joust — in Brainford with a woman?

"It is a lie!"

He then asked his wife:

"What old bawd tells thee this? By God's death, it is a lie!"

"The 'old bawd' is one who to thy face shall justify all that I speak," Mistress Openwork said.

The "old bawd" is Goshawk.

"By God's soul, do but name that rascal!" Openwork said.

"No, sir, I will not," Mistress Openwork answered.

Goshawk said to himself, "Keep thee there, girl, then!"

Openwork asked Mistress Gallipot, "Sister, do you know this varlet?"

The "varlet" was Goshawk.

"Yes," Mistress Gallipot answered.

Openwork said:

"Swear truly.

"Is there a rogue so low damned? A second Judas?"

Judas Iscariot betrayed Jesus Christ.

Openwork continued:

"A common hangman? Cutting a man's throat? Does he do it to his face? Does he bite me behind my back? Is he a back-biter? A cur-dog? Swear if you know this hell-hound!"

A cur-dog is a worthless dog.

Cerberus is a hell-hound.

"Backbiter" was a correct description of Goshawk, who was supposed to be Openwork's friend.

"In truth I do know," Mistress Gallipot said.

"What is his name?" Openwork asked.

"Not for the world will I tell you, for if I did, you would stab him."

"Oh, brave girls — worth gold!" Goshawk said to himself.

A proverb stated, "An honest woman is worth a crown of gold."

"A word, honest Master Goshawk," Openwork said.

Pretending to be angry and frustrated at not knowing who the back-stabber was, Openwork drew his sword.

"What do you mean, sir?" Goshawk asked.

Openwork said:

"Keep off and stay back, and if the devil can give a name to this new Fury, holla it — shout it — through my ear, or wrap it up in some hid character."

Furies were avenging goddesses from Hell.

"Hid character" is a secret cypher.

Openwork continued:

"I'll ride to Oxford and watch out my eyes — stay awake — but I'll hear the brazen head speak."

Robert Greene wrote a play titled *Friar Bacon and Friar Bungay*. The Oxford scholar Friar Bacon spent seven years constructing a brass head that could tell him the secrets of the universe. Unfortunately, after all his efforts, he was exhausted and was asleep when the brass head spoke. A foolish servant who was supposed to awaken him did not.

Openwork continued:

"Or else show me just one hair of his head or beard, so that I may sample it. If I meet the fiend in my own house, I'll kill him, in the street, or at the church door: Because he seeks to untie the knot God fastens, he deserves to die there."

"The knot God fastens" is "the marriage knot."

Mistress Openwork said, "My husband titles him: He calls him what he is."

"Master Goshawk, please, sir, swear to me that you know him or that you don't know him," Openwork said. "Who tells lies about me being at Brainford to lift up a petticoat other than my wife's?"

Goshawk said, "By heaven, I don't know that man!"

That man was himself: Goshawk.

"Come, come, you lie," Mistress Openwork said.

Goshawk said to her:

"Don't you want to have all the truth out?"

He was braving it out and pretending that he wanted the backbiter caught.

Goshawk said to Openwork:

"By heaven I know no man beneath the moon who is likely to do you wrong, but if I had his name, I'd print it in text letters."

"Text letters" are large and/or capital letters.

"Print thine own then," Mistress Openwork said. "Didn't thou swear to me that he — my husband — kept his whore?"

Mistress Gallipot added, "And that in sinful Brainford they would commit that deed which our lips did water at, sir, huh?"

"Commit" is a word often paired with "adultery."

Exodus 20:14 states, "*Thou shalt not commit adultery*" (King James Version).

Mistress Openwork said to Goshawk, "Thou spider, that have woven thy cunning web in my own house to ensnare me! Haven't thou sucked nourishment even underneath this roof and turned it all to poison? Spitting it on thy friend's face, my husband, as if he were sleeping and unaware of your slander? Only to leave him ugly to my eyes so that they might glance on thee?"

"Speak," Mistress Gallipot said to Goshawk. "Are these lies?"

Goshawk hung his head and said, "My own shame defeats me."

Openwork said:

"No more; he's stung.

"Who'd think that in one body there could dwell deformity and beauty, heaven and hell?

"I see that goodness is only outside. We all set counterfeit stones — jewels — in rings of gold.

"I thought that you, Goshawk, were better than that: I thought you were a true gem."

"Pardon me," Goshawk said.

Openwork said:

"In truth, I do.

"This blemish grows in human nature, not in you,

"For man's creation sticks even moles in scorn

"On fairest cheeks. Wife, nothing is perfect born."

A "mole" is a small piece of velvet that is stuck with mastic to a face.

"I thought you had been born perfect," Mistress Openwork said.

Openwork said:

"What's this whole world but a gilt, rotten pill?

"For at the heart lies the old core still."

This is perhaps an allusion to the apple from the Garden of Eden. It can be regarded as having a golden outside and a rotten core.

"Gilt" is an edible gold-colored coating that can be used on a sweetmeat.

Openwork continued:

"I'll tell you, Master Goshawk, yes, in your eye

"I have seen wanton fire, and then to test and try

"The soundness of my judgment, I told you

"I kept a whore, made you believe it was true,

"Only to feel how your pulse beat, but find

"The world can hardly yield a perfect friend.

"Come, come, it's a trick of youth — a youthful indiscretion — and it is forgiven.

"This rub — this obstacle — put aside, our love shall run more even."

"You'll deal upon men's wives no more?" Mistress Openwork asked Goshawk.

"Deal upon" means 1) plot against, and/or 2) have sex with.

"No, you teach me a trick for that," Goshawk said. "You have taught me not to do that."

"Indeed, do not deal upon men's wives," Mistress Openwork said. "They'll overreach and get the better of thee."

"Make my house yours, sir, still," Openwork said to Goshawk.

"No," Goshawk said.

He was ashamed.

Openwork said, "I say you shall: Seeing that thus besieged the house holds out, it will never fall."

The "house" was his marriage: It was built on a solid foundation. If his marriage could withstand this, the marriage knot would never be untied.

In Homer's *Odyssey*, the bed of Odysseus and Penelope is a symbol of their deeply rooted marriage. Odysseus built the bed, and he made one of the bedposts from a deeply rooted olive tree.

Master Gallipot and Greenwit, who was disguised as a summoner, entered the scene.

A summoner notified people to appear in court.

Laxton, whose face was partially hidden, appeared at a distance.

"How are things now?" the disguised Greenwit asked.

"With me, sir?" Gallipot asked.

"Yes, with you, sir," the disguised Greenwit said. "I have gone snuffling up and down by your door this hour to watch for you."

He had been trying to sniff out Gallipot's whereabouts.

To disguise his voice, Greenwit was pretending to have a cold. Summoners, however, often had a bad reputation and some summoners had a collapsed nose due to the loss of cartilage as a result of venereal disease.

"What's the matter, husband?" Mistress Gallipot asked.

She was wondering why a summoner was talking to him.

The disguised Greenwit said, "I have caught a cold in my head, sir, by sitting up late in the Rose Tavern, but I hope you understand my speech."

"So, sir," Gallipot said.

The disguised Greenwit said, "I cite you by the name of Hippocrates Gallipot, and you by the name of Prudence Gallipot, to appear upon *Crastino*, do you see, *Crastino sancti Dunstani* this Easter Term in Bow Church."

The Latin meant "the morrow of St. Dunstan's Day." "Morrow" means "the following day." St. Dunstan's Day was May 19, and so its morrow was May 20.

Gallipot asked the disguised Greenwit:

"Where, sir?"

He then asked the others:

"What does he say?

He was having trouble understanding Greenwit's disguised speech.

The disguised Greenwit said:

"Bow, Bow Church, to answer to a libel — the plaintiff's list of charges — of precontract on the part and behalf of the said Prudence and another.

"You had best, sir, take a copy of the citation; it is only twelvepence."

"Libel of precontract" was a charge that Gallipot had married a woman who was already precontracted to marry someone else, who, of course, is supposed to be Laxton.

The citation is the written subpoena.

"A citation?" someone asked.

"You pocky-nosed rascal, what slave fees you to do this?" Gallipot asked. "What scoundrel has paid you to do this?"

"Pocky-nosed" means "having a nose that displays signs of syphilis."

Laxton, who had drawn near, said to Gallipot, "Slave? I have nothing to do with you! Do you hear, sir?"

He let his face be seen.

"Laxton, isn't it?" Goshawk asked. "What vagary — devious trick — is this?"

Gallipot said, "Trust me, I thought, sir, this storm long ago had been fully allayed and laid to rest when, if you can be reminded, I paid you the last fifteen pounds, besides the thirty you had first, for then you swore."

Laxton had gotten thirty pounds, and then fifteen more pounds, and now he was back for more.

"Tush, tush, sir, oaths!" Laxton said. "Truly, I'm yet loath to vex you. Tell you what: Add to the money I have already received and make it a total of a hundred pounds and take your belly full of her."

He was asking for fifty-five more pounds. That would make the total amount of money given to him a hundred pounds.

"A hundred pounds!" Gallipot said.

"What! A hundred pounds!" Mistress Gallipot said. "He gets none. What! A hundred pounds!"

A hundred pounds was a lot of money.

Gallipot said to his wife, Mistress Prudence Gallipot:

"Sweet Pru, be calm.

"The gentleman offers thus: If I will add to the moneys that have been paid in the past and make them a hundred pounds, he will discharge all courts and give his bond never to vex us more. He will stop all his lawsuits and sign a legal agreement not to bring these lawsuits against us again."

Mistress Gallipot said:

"A hundred pounds! Alas!"

She then said to Laxton:

"Take, sir, just threescore pounds. Do you seek my undoing and ruination?"

Threescore pounds are sixty pounds. Laxton had already received forty-five pounds, so he would receive fifteen more pounds.

"I'll not abate — deduct — one sixpence," Laxton said. "I'll maul you, puss, for spitting."

"Do thy worst!" Mistress Gallipot said. "Will fourscore pounds stop thy mouth?"

"No," Laxton said.

Mistress Gallipot said:

"You are a slave! Thou cheat, I'll now tear money from thy throat!

"Husband, lay hold on yonder tawny-coat."

Summoners wore tawny coats.

"Nay, gentlemen, seeing your women are so hot and angry, I must lose my hair in their company, I see," the disguised Greenwit said.

Greenwit removed his wig.

"His hair sheds off, and yet he does not speak as much in the nose as he did before," Mistress Openwork said.

People who had syphilis lost their hair and lost the cartilage in their nose, resulting in its collapse.

Mistress Openwork was joking that she was surprised that the "syphilis" that had caused his hair loss had also improved his nose.

Goshawk said:

"He has had the better chirurgeon — the better surgeon — who has cured him.

"Master Greenwit, is your wit so raw as to play no better a part than a summoner's?"

Conmen sometimes learned a little law and then pretended to be summoners.

Gallipot said, "I ask, who plays *A Knack to Know an Honest Man* in this company?"

A Knack to Know an Honest Man was the title of a 1594 play.

Gallipot wanted to know who was an honest man in this group of people.

"Dear husband, pardon me, I did dissemble and deceive you, when I told thee that I was his precontracted wife, when letters came from him asking for thirty pounds," Mistress Gallipot said. "I had no shift but that. That was my only deception to you."

"A very clean shift, but able to make me lousy," Gallipot said. "Go on."

He suspected that he was a cuckold: a man with an unfaithful wife.

A shift is 1) an article of clothing, or 2) a trick.

"Lousy" means infested with lice.

Lice is much less a problem these days than it was then. Antoni Van Leeuwenhoek (1632-1723) did not invent the microscope, but he was the first to use it to see bacteria, red blood cells, and sperm cells. He was curious to see as much as possible and to study carefully as many things as possible through the microscope. Many of the insects he wished to study could be found around his home, such as fleas and mites. However, when he wanted to study lice, he had to buy some. They weren't difficult to buy. He wrote, "I had plenty of them brought to me for my money."

"Husband, I plucked, when he had tempted me to think well of him, gelt feathers from thy wings to make him fly loftier," Mistress Gallipot said.

She had found a way to give Laxton money.

"Fly to on top of you, wife," Gallipot said. "Go on."

He was more certain that he was a cuckold.

"He, having wasted them, comes now for more, using me as a ruffian — a pimp — does his whore, whose sin keeps him in breath — alive — by means of the money she makes," Mistress Gallipot said. "By heaven I vow thy bed he never wronged, more than he does now."

Gallipot said:

"Not wronged my bed? Ha, ha, likely enough. A shop-board will serve to have a cuckold's coat cut out upon it."

A shop-board is a table or counter for conducting business or displaying goods.

Gallipot still believed that he had been cuckolded. Laxton had not wronged his bed; instead, he could have had sex with Gallipot's wife on a shop-board. It was Gallipot's shop-board that had been wronged.

Gallipot continued:

"Of that we'll talk hereafter. You are a villain."

"Just hear me speak, sir," Laxton said. "You shall find that I am not a villain."

Someone said, "Please, sir, be patient and hear him."

"I am muzzled against biting, sir," Gallipot said to Laxton. "Treat me how you will."

Laxton said:

"The first hour that your wife was in my eye, I myself was with other gentlemen sitting by in your shop tasting smoke — that is, we were smoking — and speech was being used.

"Someone stated that men who have the fairest wives are most abused and with difficulty escape the horn."

In other words: Only with difficulty would they escape being cuckolded. (Cuckolds were said to have invisible horns growing on their forehead.)

Laxton continued:

"Your wife maintained that such spots in the reputation of city dames were justly stained only if they were not made by men's slanders."

In other words: Some women lost their good reputations only because of the slander of men.

Laxton continued:

"As for her own part, she vowed that you had so much of her heart that no man by all his wit, by any wile no matter how fine spun, should beguile yourself of what in her was yours."

In other words: She said that no man would cheat you out of what was yours — your wife's heart.

Gallipot said to his wife:

"Yet, Pru, it is well."

He then said to Laxton:

"Play out your game at Irish, sir. Finish your story. Who wins?"

"Irish" is a dice game similar to backgammon.

"The trial is when she comes to bearing," Mistress Openwork said.

"Bearing" can mean "child-bearing" and the bearing of the weight of a man during sex. It can also refer to the removal of a piece at the end of a game of Irish.

Laxton said:

"I scorned that one woman should thus brave — defy — all men, and, which more vexed me, that one woman was a she-citizen — a city woman. I did not believe that that was possible.

"Therefore, I laid siege to her; she held out, gave me many a brave repulse, and compelled me with shame to sound retreat to my hot lust.

"Then, seeing all my base desires raked up in dust and smothered like a fire dampened with ashes, and seeing that I swore never to presume again to tempt her modest ears, she said that her eyes would always give me welcome honestly, and since I was a gentleman, if my finances ran low, she would relieve my state, as long as it would not overthrow your own and her finances; she did so.

"Then, seeing that I wrought upon her meekness and compassion, she set me at nought and despised me. And you see what stream and current I yet strove with to see if I could turn that tide.

"But, sir, I swear by heaven, and by those hopes men lay up there, I neither have nor had a base intent to wrong your bed; what has been done is merriment.

"Your gold I pay back with this interest: When I had the most power to do it, I wronged you least."

Gallipot said, "If this is no gullery and trickery, sir —"

"No, no, on my life!" Laxton said.

Can we believe part of Laxton's story?

Is he telling a tale to make the best of an uncomfortable situation?

Is he really paying back the gold? Or is the "interest" his payment for the gold?

It seems unlikely that he paid back the gold; however, it seems likely that he did not sleep with Mistress Gallipot although she may have wanted to sleep with him.

Gallipot said:

"Then, sir, I am beholden and indebted not to you, wife.

"But, Master Laxton, I am beholden and indebted to your lack of doing ill, which it seems you have not.

"Gentlemen, all of you tarry and dine here."

Openwork said to Gallipot, "Brother, we have a jest — a humorous narrative — as good as yours to furnish out — enhance — a feast."

"We'll crown our table with it," Gallipot said. "Wife, brag no more of holding out: She who most brags is most whore."

They exited.

CHAPTER 5

— 5.1 —

Jack Dapper, Moll Cutpurse, Sir Beauteous Ganymede, and Sir Thomas Long talked together on a street.

Jack Dapper said, "But please, Master Captain Jack, be plain and perspicuous — speak clearly — with me. Was it your Meg of Westminster's courage that rescued me from the Poultry puttocks indeed?"

Master Captain Jack was Moll Cutpurse, who was wearing male attire. "Jack" is a name used to refer to any man, but Moll may have used it when she was wearing masculine attire.

Meg of Westminster was another, earlier roaring girl, who was much like Moll Cutpurse. Her story is told in *The Life and Pranks of Long Meg of Westminster* (1582).

"Poultry puttocks" are officers at the Poultry Counter: the debtors' prison on Poultry Street.

Literally, puttocks are certain kinds of birds of prey, including buzzards.

Moll Cutpurse said, "The valor of my wit, I assure you, sir, fetched and rescued you off bravely when you were in the forlorn hope among those desperates. Sir Beauteous Ganymede here and Sir Thomas Long heard that foolish cuckoo, my serving-man Trapdoor, sing the note of your ransom from captivity."

"Forlorn hope" was a phrase used to describe the body of men who were chosen to lead an attack and so were in the most dangerous position of a battle.

"By God's soul, Moll, where's that Trapdoor?" Sir Beauteous Ganymede asked.

"Hanged, I think, by this time," Moll Cutpurse said. "A justice in this town who speaks nothing but 'make a *mittimus*; away with him to Newgate' used that rogue like a firework — a firecracker — to run upon a line between him and me."

The justice of the peace she was talking about was Sir Alexander.

A mittimus was a writ for keeping someone in custody.

The rogue was Trapdoor.

Newgate was a prison.

"What! What!" the people present said.

Moll Cutpurse said:

"By the Virgin Mary, the justice wanted to lay trains of villainy to blow up my life."

The trains were figurative lines of gunpowder that would be lit at one end and burn down to set off the explosive.

Moll Cutpurse continued:

"I smelled the powder, spied what linstock gave fire to shoot against the poor captain of the galley-foist, and I slid away my serving-man, like a shovel-board shilling."

Moll Cutpurse was describing in figurative words the traps that Sir Alexander had set for her. She had gotten rid of Trapdoor, knowing or suspecting that he had helped Sir Alexander, who wanted to blow up her life.

A linstock was a long stick that held a match used to fire a cannon. Trapdoor was the figurative linstock.

Moll was figuratively "the poor captain of the galley-foist," which is literally a flat-bottomed boat with oars. On state occasions, the Lord Mayor of London used a galley-barge. A barge is a flat-bottomed boat. A galley-barge is not a proper target — certainly not when the Lord Mayor of London is on it.

According to the *Oxford English Dictionary*, a "foist" is "A cheat, a rogue; a pick-pocket."

Shovel-board shillings were used in the game of shuffleboard.

Moll Cutpurse continued:

"He — Trapdoor — struts up and down the suburbs, I think, and eats up whores, feeds upon a bawd's garbage."

Moll believed that Trapdoor was now living off the earnings of whores.

"Sirrah Jack Dapper," Sir Thomas Long said.

"What does Tom Long say?" Jack Dapper asked.

"Thou had a sweet-faced boy, hail-fellow with thee in your little Gull," Sir Thomas Long said. "How is he spent? What is he doing now?"

Jack Dapper said:

"Indeed, I whistled the poor little buzzard off of my fist because when he waited upon me at the ordinaries, the gallants hit me in the teeth — that is, made fun of me — always, and said I looked like an alderman's painted tomb, and the boy at my elbow like a death's head."

"Whistled him off" means "dismissed him by whistling." This is done in falconry.

"Ordinaries" are eating-places.

The tombs of aldermen were often showily painted and included a *memento mori* such as a skull.

Jack Dapper then said to Moll Cutpurse:

"Sirrah Jack, Moll."

"What says my little Dapper?" Moll Cutpurse asked.

"Come, come, walk and talk, walk and talk," Sir Beauteous Ganymede said.

"Moll and I'll be in the middle," Jack Dapper said.

Moll Cutpurse said:

"These knights shall have squires' places, perhaps, then."

Sir Beauteous Ganymede and Sir Thomas Long would walk on the outsides with Moll and Jack Dapper on the inside. Normally, lower-ranking squires would be on the outside.

Moll then said:

"Well, Dapper, what do you say?"

"Sirrah Captain Mad Mary, the gull my own father, Dapper Sir Davy, laid these London boot-halers, the catchpoles, in ambush to set upon and attack me," Jack Dapper said.

A "gull" is a fool.

"Boot-halers" are highwaymen.

"Catch-poles" are arresting officers.

One of the people around him said, "Your father? Get out, Jack! I don't believe you!"

"By the tassels of this handkerchief, it is true," Jack Dapper said. "And what was his warlike stratagem, do you think? He thought because a wicker cage tames a nightingale, a lousy prison could make an ass of me."

"A nasty plot," one of the people around him said.

"Aye, as though a counter, which is a park in which all the wild beasts of the city run head by head, could tame me," Jack Dapper said.

Lord Noland entered the scene.

Seeing him, Moll Cutpurse said, "Yonder comes my Lord Noland."

"May God save you, my lord," everyone said to Lord Noland.

"Well met, gentlemen all, good Sir Beauteous Ganymede, Sir Thomas Long," Lord Noland said. "And how does Master Dapper?"

"Thanks, my lord," Jack Dapper said.

"No tobacco, my lord?" Moll Cutpurse asked.

She was offering him a smoke.

"No, indeed, Jack," Lord Noland said.

"My Lord Noland, will you go to the Pimlico Inn with us?" Jack Dapper asked. "We are making a boon voyage to that nappy — that heady — land of spice-cakes."

A "boon voyage" is a *bon voyage*.

"Here's such a merry ging — a merry gang — that I could find in my heart to sail to the world's end with such company," Lord Noland said. "Come, gentlemen, let's go on."

Some taverns on the outskirts of London were named The World's End.

They walked.

"Here's most amorous weather, my lord," Jack Dapper said.

"Amorous weather?" the others asked.

Jack Dapper may have meant lovely weather.

"Isn't 'amorous' a good word?" Jack Dapper asked.

Trapdoor, disguised like a poor soldier with a patch over one eye, and Tearcat entered the scene. Both were wearing tattered clothing and carrying cudgels. Both were pretending to be former military men. They were trying to get people to pity them and give them money. Or they were trying to get people to be afraid of the cudgels and give them money.

Trapdoor said to Tearcat:

"Shall we set upon the infantry, these troops of foot?"

He was going to "attack" the four people coming toward them with his fraudulent begging.

Then he recognized Moll Cutpurse:

"By God's wounds, yonder comes Moll, my whorish master and mistress! I wish that I had her kidneys between my teeth."

Tearcat said, "I had rather have a cow-heel between my teeth."

He was hungry.

A cow-heel is an item of food: It is a cow's foot that has been cooked until it turns into a jelly.

"By God's wounds, I am so patched up that she cannot discover and recognize my identity," Trapdoor said. "We'll go on."

He was wearing a patch over his eye and patches on his clothing. Probably, he had one or more bandages.

"*Alla corago* then," Tearcat said.

Coraggio is Italian for "courage."

Alla coraggio means "to courage."

Trapdoor addressed Moll Cutpurse and her companions, "Your good honors and worships, enlarge the ears of commiseration and let the sound of a hoarse military organ-pipe penetrate your pitiful — your full-of-pity — bowels to extract out of them so many small drops of silver as may give a hard straw-bed lodging to a couple of maimed soldiers."

He was begging for silver coins.

"Where are you maimed?" Jack Dapper asked.

"In both our nether limbs," Tearcat said.

"Nether limbs" can be 1) legs, or 2) penises.

Moll Cutpurse said:

"Come, come, Dapper, let's give them something.

"Alas, poor men, what money do you have? By my truth, I love a soldier with my soul."

"Wait, wait, where have you served?" Sir Beauteous Ganymede asked.

"In any part of the Low Countries?" Sir Thomas Long asked.

Trapdoor answered, "Not in the Low Countries, if it please your manhood, but in Hungary against the Turk — the Sultan Solyman the Magnificent — at the siege of Belgrade."

In 1521, the Hungarians lost Belgrade, the capital of Serbia, to the Turks. The siege of Belgrade lasted 25 June-29 August 1521.

The Roaring Girl was written around 1607-1610, and so the disguised Trapdoor was much too young to have served during the siege of Belgrade.

"Who served there with you, sirrah?" Lord Noland said.

Trapdoor answered, "Many Hungarians, Moldavians, Walachians, and Transylvanians, with some Sclavonians, and retiring home, sir, the Venetian galleys took us prisoners, yet freed us and allowed us to beg up and down the country."

"You have ambled all over Italy then?" Jack Dapper asked.

Trapdoor answered, "Oh, sir, from Venice to Roma, Vecchio, Bononia, Romania, Bolonia, Modena, Piacenza, and Tuscana with all her cities, as Pistoia, Valteria, Mountepulchena, Arezzo with the Siennois, and diverse others."

"These are mere rogues," Moll Cutpurse said. "Put spurs to them once more. Chase them away."

From his answers, Moll Cutpurse realized that the disguised Trapdoor was merely making up the "facts" of his life. A problem in this society was some con men pretended to be disabled soldiers so that people would give them money.

Jack Dapper said to Tearcat:

"Thou look like a strange creature, a fat butter-box, yet thou speak English."

A stereotype of the Dutch people is that they loved butter and were fat.

Jack Dapper then asked:

"Who are thou?"

Tearcat then tried to convince Jack Dapper and the others that he was Dutch:

"Ick, mine here? Ick bin den ruffling Tearcat, den brave soldado. Ick bin dorick all Dutchlant gueresen. Der shellum das meere ine beasa ine woert gaeb, Ick slaag um stroakes on tom cop, dastick den hundred touzun divell. halle. Frollick, mine here."

The "ruffling Tearcat" is the "swaggering Tearcat."

Tearcat's mangled "Dutch" was saying, roughly:

"I, my lord? I am the ruffling Tearcat, the brave soldier. I have traveled through all Dutchland. The rascal who gave an angry word, I beat him with blows on the head, pulled out thence a hundred thousand devils. Cheerful, my lord."

Tearcat's "Dutch" is so mangled that Google Translate identified it as Krio, which is an English-based Creole language of Sierra Leone in Africa.

Sir Beauteous Ganymede said, "Here, here, let's be rid of their jobbering and their jabbering."

He wanted to give them a few coins to get rid of them.

According to the *Oxford English Dictionary*, a "jobber" is "A person who [...] pecks, posts, thrusts, etc."

These beggars were bothering and picking and jabbering at them in hopes to get a few coins.

Moll Cutpurse said:

"We won't give them even a cross, Sir Beauteous."

A "cross" is a penny, a coin on which a cross was stamped.

Moll then said to the disguised Trapdoor and to Tearcat:

"You base rogues, I have taken measure of you better than a tailor can, and I'll fit you as you, monster with one eye, have fitted me."

In other words: I'll treat you as you have treated me.

They had treated her badly with their fraudulent begging.

The "monster with one eye" was the disguised Trapdoor, who was wearing a patch over one eye.

A "monster with one eye" may be a penis.

"Your worship will not abuse a soldier?" Trapdoor asked.

"Soldier?" Moll Cutpurse said. "Thou deserve to be hanged up by that tongue which dishonors so noble a profession. Soldier, you skeldering — you sponging — varlet! Hold, stand, there should be a trapdoor hereabouts."

She pulled off Trapdoor's eyepatch.

Trapdoor said, "The balls of these glaziers of mine — that is, my eyes — shall be shot up and down in any hot piece of service for my invincible mistress."

In other words: His eyeballs would be like cannonballs shot in Moll's service. They would search for ways for him to serve her.

A "hot piece of service" can be an energetic bout of sex.

"I did not think there had been such knavery in black patches, as now I see," Jack Dapper said.

The disguised Trapdoor and Tearcat were wearing black patches — bandages — to make it seem as though they had been injured in battle.

Moll Cutpurse said to Jack Dapper about Trapdoor, "Oh, sir, he has been brought up in the Isle of Dogs, and he can both fawn like a spaniel and bite like a mastiff as he finds occasion."

The Isle of Dogs was a peninsula in the Thames River.

Lord Noland asked Tearcat, "Who are you, sirrah? A bird of this feather, too?"

"I am a man beaten from the wars, sir," Tearcat said.

He meant that the wars had beaten him down.

"I think so, for you never stood to fight," Sir Thomas Long said.

He meant that Tearcat had been beaten because he was a deserter.

"What's thy name, fellow soldier?" Jack Dapper asked Tearcat, who was Trapdoor's fellow soldier.

He replied, "I am called Tearcat by those who have seen my valor."

"Tearcat?" someone asked.

To "tear a cat" means to "bluster." Tearcats can be bullies and swaggerers.

Moll Cutpurse said:

"A mere whip-jack, and that is, in the commonwealth of rogues, a slave who can talk of sea-fights, name all your chief pirates, discover and talk about more countries to you than either the Dutch or Spanish or French or English ever found out, yet indeed all his service is by land, and that is to rob a fair or some such venturous exploit."

A "whip-jack" was a man who pretended to be a down-on-his-luck sailor.

Thomas Dekker wrote a series of pamphlets about conmen. In 1599, he had been imprisoned in the Poultry Counter as a debtor. According to his *The Bellman of London*, whip-jacks are a "sort of nimble-fing'red knaves [...] who talk of nothing but fights at sea, piracies, drownings and shipwracks, travelling both in the shapes and names of mariners, with a counterfeit license to beg from town to town [...]. The end of their land voyage is to rob booths at fairs [...]. These whip-jacks will talk of the Indies and of all countries that lie under heaven, but are indeed no more than fresh-water soldiers."

Moll Cutpurse continued:

"Tearcat! By God's foot, sirrah, I have your name now! I remember, in my book of horners, horns for the thumb, you know how."

"Horners" work with horns as a material. Or they can be cuckold-makers.

"Horns for the thumb" are thimbles made for the thumb. Cutpurses — thieves — used them to protect their thumbs when cutting the strings of a purse.

Tearcat said:

"No, indeed, Captain Moll, for I know you by sight: I am no such nipping — purse-cutting — Christian. But I am a maunderer upon the pad — a beggar upon the road — I confess.

"Meeting with honest Trapdoor here, whom you had cashiered from bearing arms, out at elbows under your colors, I instructed him in the rudiments of roguery, and by my map made him sail over any country you can name, so that now he can maunder better than myself."

"Cashiered from bearing arms" meant that Moll had fired him.

"Out at elbows" meant "poor and ragged," as in wearing a coat whose elbows have worn out and have holes.

"Under your colors" means "wearing your livery."

"Livery" is the distinctive clothing worn by a servant that showed by whom he was employed.

Tearcat had taught Trapdoor how to be a rogue. For example, he had taught Trapdoor the names of geographical locations such as those he had rattled off earlier as evidence that he had traveled.

"So then, Trapdoor, thou are turned soldier now," Jack Dapper said.

"Alas, sir, now there's no wars, it is the safest course of life I could take," Trapdoor said.

"I hope then you can cant, for by your cudgels, you, sirrah, are an upright man," Moll Cutpurse said.

"Cant" is the jargon — the specialized language — of conmen. They used it to communicate among themselves without other people understanding.

According to Thomas Dekker's *Lanthorn and Candlelight*, "It was necessary that a people, so fast increasing and so daily practicing new and strange villainies, should borrow to themselves a speech which, so near as they could, none but themselves could understand; and for that cause was this language, which some call pedlar's French, invented [...]. This word 'canting' seems to be derived from the Latin verb *canto*, which signifies in English to sing, or to make a sound with words, that's to say, speak. And very aptly may 'canting' take [its] derivation *a cantando*, from singing, because amongst these beggarly consorts that can play upon no better instruments, the language of canting is a kind of music, and he that [who] in such assemblies can cant best is [ac]counted the best musician."

An upright man is a strong man who carries a cudgel. When an upright man begs, people give him money because they are afraid of him.

"I am as upright as anyone who walks the highway, I assure you," Trapdoor said.

"And Tearcat, what are you?" Moll Cutpurse asked. "A wild rogue, an angler, or a ruffler?"

A "wild rogue" was born and raised in the lifestyle of a rogue. A "wild rogue" is a born rogue.

An angler used a pole with a hook at the end to fish through open windows for what he could steal.

Upright men are at the top of the hierarchy of rogues.

Rufflers are near the top of the hierarchy of rogues.

"Brother to this upright man, flesh and blood, ruffling Tearcat is my name, and a ruffler is my style, my title, my profession," Tearcat said.

"Sirrah, where's your doxy?" Moll Cutpurse said. "Don't halt with me. Don't lie to me."

A "halt" is a limp. Moll was telling him to be straightforward with her and not hesitate to think about which lie to tell: Instead, just tell her the truth.

A beggar could pretend to limp to get sympathetic people to give him money.

"Doxy, Moll?" someone asked. "What's that?"

"His wench," Moll answered.

Using cant in his answer, Trapdoor said:

"My doxy? [wench?] I have, by the salomon [mass], a doxy who carries a kinchin mort [little girl] in her slate [sheet] at her back, besides my dell and my dainty wild dell, with all of whom I'll tumble [have sex with] this next darkmans [night] in the strommel [straw], and drink ben [good] booze, and eat a fat gruntling cheat, a cackling cheat, and a quacking cheat."

According to Thomas Dekker's *The Bellman of London*, "Kinchin morts are girls of a year or two old, which the morts, their mothers, carry at their backs in the slates, which in the canting tongue are sheets."

Also according to Dekker's *The Bellman of London*, "A dell is a young wench [...] but as yet not spoiled of her maidenhead [...]. These dells are reserved as dishes for the upright men, for none but they must have the first taste of them."

A dell is a young woman who is not sexually experienced; a doxy is a woman who is sexually experienced.

"Wild dells" were begotten and born under hedges. They were born into the rogue lifestyle.

A "cheat" is a "thing."

"A gruntling cheat, a cackling cheat, and a quacking cheat" is a pig, a chicken, and a duck.

"Here's plenteous and fine cheating," Jack Dapper said.

"My doxy stays for me in a boozing ken, brave captain," Trapdoor said.

A "ken" is a house, and a "boozing ken" is an alehouse.

Moll Cutpurse said to Jack Dapper:

"He says his wench waits for him in an alehouse."

She then said to Trapdoor and Tearcat:

"You are no pure rogues."

Moll may have meant that they were not complete rogues. Trapdoor, for one, was new at begging, being taught by Tearcat. Also, so far they had confessed only to begging, and beggars are not complete rogues, but Tearcat will now say that they are receivers of stolen goods.

Interpreting "pure" to mean "morally pure," Tearcat said. "Pure rogues? No, we scorn to be pure rogues, but if you come to our libken [lodgings], or our stalling ken [house for receiving stolen goods], you shall find neither him nor me a queer cuffin."

According to Thomas Dekker's *Lanthorn and Candlelight*, "The word *cove* or *cofe* or *cuffin* signifies a man, a fellow, etc., but differs something [somewhat] in his property according as it meets with other words, for a gentleman is called a *gentry cove* or *cofe*, a good fellow is a *ben cofe*, a churl is called a *queer cuffin* [...] and in canting they term a Justice of the Peace (because he punisheth them, belike) by no other name than by *queer cuffin*, that's to say a churl or a naughty man."

"So, sir, you are not a churl," Moll Cutpurse said.

So, he was not a justice of the peace.

"No, but I am a ben cove, a brave cove, a gentry cuffin," Tearcat said.

"Do you call this canting?" Lord Noland asked.

"By God's wounds, I'll give a schoolmaster half a crown a week, if he will teach me this pedlar's French," Jack Dapper said.

"Pedlar's French" is another name for "cant."

"Do but stroll, sir, half a harvest with us, sir, and you shall gabble your bellyful," Trapdoor said.

In other words: Spend half a harvest season of begging and thieving with us, and you can talk your fill of cant.

"Come, you rogue, cant with me," Moll Cutpurse said.

Sir Thomas Long said:

"Well said, Moll."

He then said to Cutpurse:

"Cant with her, sirrah, and you shall have money, else not a penny."

"I'll have a bout if she please," Trapdoor said.

"Come on, sirrah," Moll Cutpurse said.

Trapdoor said, "Ben mort [Good woman], shall you and I heave [rob] a booth, mill [rob] a ken [house], or nip a bung [purse]? And then we'll couch a hogshead [lie down and sleep] under the ruffmans [woods or bushes], and there you shall wap [have sex] with me, and I'll niggle [have sex] with you."

Slapping and kicking him, Moll Cutpurse said, "Get out, you damned, impudent rascal!"

Trapdoor said, "Cut benar whids [Speak good words], and hold back your fambles [hands] and your stamps [legs]."

"Nay, nay, Moll, why are thou angry?" Lord Noland asked. "What was his gibberish?"

Moll Cutpurse, who knew cant well, said:

"By the Virgin Mary, this, my lord, says he:

"Ben mort.

"This means: Good wench.

"Shall you and I heave a booth, mill a ken, or nip a bung?

"This means: Shall you and I rob a booth or house or shall we cut a purse?"

"Very good," the others said.

Moll Cutpurse then said:

"And then we'll couch a hogshead under the ruffmans.

"This means: And then we'll lie under a hedge."

Trapdoor said, "That was my desire, captain, as it is fitting a soldier should lie."

"And there you shall wap with me and I'll niggle with you, and that's all!" Moll Cutpurse said.

"Nay, nay, Moll, what's that 'wap'?" Sir Beauteous Ganymede said.

"Nay, teach me what 'niggling' is," Jack Dapper said. "I'd like to be niggling."

"Wapping and niggling is all one," Moll Cutpurse said. "The rogue my serving-man can tell you."

Trapdoor said, "It is fadoodling [having sex], if it please you."

Sir Beauteous Ganymede said:

"This is excellent."

He then requested:

"One fit more, good Moll."

A "fit" is a piece of music. This word is not cant.

Moll said to Tearcat:

"Come, you rogue, sing with me."

She sang:

"*A gage of ben rom-booze*"

[A quart-pot of good wine]

"*In a boozing ken of Romville*"

[In a tavern of London]

Tearcat sang:

"*Is benar than a caster,*"

[Is better than a cloak,]

"*Peck, pannam, lap, or popler,*"

[Meat, bread, butter, or porridge,]

"*Which we mill in deuse a vill.*"

[Which we steal in the country.]

Moll and Tearcat sang together:

"*Oh, I would lib all the lightmans,* "

[Oh, I would lie all the day,]

"*Oh, I would lib all the darkmans,*"

[Oh, I would lie all the night,]

"*By the salomon, under the ruffmans,*"

[By the mass, under the bushes,]

"*By the salomon, in the hartmans!*"

[By the mass, in the stocks!]"

Tearcat sang:

"*And scour the queer cramp-ring,*"

[And wear fetters, aka handcuffs,]

"*And couch till a palliard docked with my dell,*"

[And sleep until a beggar had sex with my wench,]

"*So my boozy nab might skew rom-booze well.*"

[So long as my boozy head might drink good wine well.]

Moll and Tearcat sang together:

"*Avast to the pad, let us bing,*"

[Away to the highway, let us go,]

"*Avast to the pad, let us bing.*"

[Away to the highway, let us go.]

"These are fine knaves, indeed!" someone said.

Jack Dapper said:

"The grating of ten new cartwheels and the gruntling of five hundred hogs coming from Romford hog market cannot make a worse noise than this canting language does in my ears.

"Please, my Lord Noland, let's give these soldiers their pay."

"Agreed, and let them march," Sir Beauteous Ganymede said.

Giving her money, Lord Noland said, "Here, Moll."

Moll Cutpurse said to Trapdoor and Tearcat:

"Now I see that you are installed — ordained — into the society of rogues and are not ashamed of your professions."

She gave Trapdoor and Tearcat the money and said:

"Look, my Lord Noland here and these gentlemen bestow upon you two, two bords and a half — that's two shillings sixpence."

"Thanks to your lordship," Trapdoor said.

"Thanks, heroical captain," Tearcat said.

"Go now," Moll Cutpurse said to Trapdoor and Tearcat.

"We shall cut ben whids — we shall speak well — about your masters and mistress-ship wheresoever we go," Trapdoor said.

"You'll maintain, sirrah, the old justice's plot to his face?" Moll Cutpurse asked. "You'll tell the truth about Sir Alexander's plot to his face?"

Trapdoor replied, "If I don't, then trine [hang] me on the cheats [gallows] — hang me."

"Be sure you meet me there," Moll Cutpurse said.

"Without any more begging, I'll do it," Trapdoor said. "Follow, brave Tearcat."

Tearcat said:

"*I prae, sequor.*"

The Latin means: Go before, I follow.

He then said to Trapdoor:

"Let us go, mouse."

"Mouse" is a term of affection.

Trapdoor and Tearcat exited.

"Moll, what was in that canting song?" Lord Noland asked.

Moll said:

"Indeed, my lord, it was only a praise of good drink, the only milk that these wild beasts love to suck, and thus it was:

"*A rich cup of wine,*

"*Oh, it is juice divine,*

"*More wholesome for the head*

"*Than meat, drink, or bread*

"*To fill my drunken pate*!

"*With that, I'd sit up late;*

"*By the heels would I lie,*

"*Under a lousy hedge die.*

"*Let a slave have a pull [have sex]*

"*At [with] my whore, so [as long as] I be [am] full*

"*Of that precious liquor —*

"And a parcel of such stuff, my lord, not worth the opening and explaining."

Some people entered the scene, including a cutpurse very gallantly and finely dressed, with four or five other cutpurses after him. One of the men was carrying a wand: a switch for use on horses, or a light walking stick.

"What gallant comes yonder?" Lord Noland asked.

"By the mass, I think I know him," Sir Thomas Long said. "He is from Cumberland."

Cumberland is a northern county.

The first cutpurse said to the others, "Shall we venture to shuffle in among yonder heap of gallants and strike?"

"To strike" meant "to commit a theft."

"It is a question whether there are any silver shells [coins] among them for all their satin outsides," the second cutpurse said.

Certainly that was true of the gallantly dressed cutpurse.

"Let's try," another cutpurse said.

Moll Cutpurse said, "A pox on him! A gallant? Shadow me and follow me closely. I know him: He is one who encumbers the land, indeed; if he swims near to the shore of any of your pockets, look to your purses."

"Is it possible?" someone in Moll's group asked.

"This splendidly dressed fellow is no better than a foist," Moll Cutpurse said.

"Foist?" someone in Moll's group asked. "What's that?"

Moll Cutpurse said:

"A foist is a diver with two fingers: a pickpocket. All his train of followers study the figging law, that's to say, the cutting of purses and foisting."

The figging law is the code and craft of the cutpurse and pickpocket.

Moll Cutpurse continued:

"One of them is a nip; I took him once in the twopenny gallery at the Fortune."

The nip is the person who cuts the purse and picks the pocket. The nip then hands the booty to another person.

Moll had once seen the first cutpurse in the act of stealing a purse.

The Fortune is the theater where *The Roaring Girl* was first performed.

Moll Cutpurse continued:

"Then there's a cloyer, or snap, who dogs any new brother in that trade, and snaps will have half in any booty.

"He with the wand is both a stale, whose office is to face a man in the streets while shells — coins — are drawn out of his pocket by another —"

A stale is a decoy who distracts the person being stolen from face to face.

Moll Cutpurse continued:

"— and then with his black conjuring rod in his hand, he, by the nimbleness of his eye and juggling-stick, will in cheaping [bargaining for] a piece of plate at a goldsmith's stall, make four or five rings mount from the top of his caduceus [wand], and, as if it were at leap-frog, they skip into his hand presently."

Thieves would find a way to steal four or five rings by sliding them down a thin walking stick or a riding switch, or by sliding them off the baton on which the goldsmith displayed the rings.

Mercury, the god of thieves, carried a caduceus.

According to Thomas Dekker's *The Bellman of London*:

"This figging law, like the body of some monstrous and terrible beast, stands upon ten feet, or rather lifts up proudly ten dragon-like heads, the names of which are these, *viz.*:

"He that cuts the purse is called the nip.

"He that is half with him is the snap, or the cloyer.

"The knife is called a cuttle-bung.

"He that picks the pocket is called a foist.

"He that faceth the man is the stale.

"The taking of the purse is called drawing.

"The spying of this villain is called smoking or boiling.

"The purse is the bung.

"The money [is] the shells.

"The act doing is called striking."

"By God's wounds, we are smoked out and detected!" the second cutpurse said. "She knows what we are!"

"Huh?" a cutpurse said.

"We are boiled and done for," the second cutpurse said. "A pox on her! See, Moll, the roaring drab — the roaring whore!"

"May all the diseases of sixteen hospitals boil her!" the first cutpurse said. "Let's go away!"

Syphilis was treated with hot baths.

Some diseases cause boils.

"Bless you, sir," Moll Cutpurse said.

"And you, good sir," the first cutpurse said.

"Don't you ken — know — me, man?" Moll Cutpurse asked.

"No, trust me, sir," the first cutpurse said. "Believe me, sir."

"By God's heart, there's a knight to whom I'm bound for many favors who lost his purse at the last new play in the Swan Theater, with seven angels in it," Moll Cutpurse said. "Make it good; it would be best for you. Do you see? No more."

Moll was going to make the first cutpurse return the seven angels she had seen him steal.

"A synagogue shall be called, Mistress Mary, to find out who took the purse; don't disgrace me," the first cutpurse said. "*Pacus palabros*, I will conjure for you. Farewell."

He did not want to be disgraced by being revealed to be a cutpurse while he was wearing gallants' clothing.

A synagogue is a meeting of thieves.

Pacus palabras comes from the Spanish *pocas palabras*, which means "few words."

The first cutpurse was going to conjure up seven angels to be returned to the knight.

The cutpurses exited.

"Didn't I tell you, my lord?" Moll Cutpurse said.

"I wonder how thou came to know these nasty villains," Lord Noland said.

"And why do the foul mouths of the world call thee Moll Cutpurse?" Sir Thomas Long said. "A name, I think, damned and odious."

Moll Cutpurse said:

"Does anyone dare to step forth to my face and say, 'I have caught thee taking a purse, Moll'?

"I must confess that in my younger days, when I was apt to stray, I have sat among such adders, seen their stings as any here might, and in full playhouses watched their quick-diving hands to bring to shame such rogues, and in that stream, I met an ill name.

"When next, my lord, you spy any one of those, as long as he is in his art a scholar — an expert thief — question him, tempt him with gold to open the large book of his close villainies, and you yourself shall cant better than poor Moll can, and know more laws of cheaters, lifters, nips, foists, puggards, curbers, with all the devil's black guard, than it is fit should be discovered to a noble wit."

Thomas Dekker writes in *The Bellman of London*, "The cheating law, or the art of winning money by false dice. Those that practise this study call themselves cheaters, the dice cheaters, and the money which they purchase [make] cheats."

Dekker also writes in *The Bellman of London*:

The lifting law "teacheth a kind of lifting of goods clean away. The such liftings are three sorts of levers used to get up the baggage, *viz.*:

"He that first stealeth the parcel is called the lift.

"[He] that receives it is the marker.

"He that stands without [outside] and carries it away is called the santar."

"Puggards" are thieves.

"Curbers" are thieves who use a stick with a hook to steal items by hooking them through a window.

A "black guard" is a guard of attendants, who in this case are black in character. Black guards are also the devil's attendants.

Moll Cutpurse continued:

"I know they have their orders, offices and official positions, circuits and circles to which they are bound and indentured to raise their own damnation in."

Sorcerers would stand in a protective circle when raising malevolent demons.

Here, the rogues were making their circles and raising only their own damnation.

"How do thou know it?" Jack Dapper asked.

Moll Cutpurse answered:

"As you do: I show it to you, they show it to me."

She then asked Lord Noland:

"Suppose, my lord, you were in Venice."

"Well," Lord Noland said.

"If some Italian pander — pimp — there would tell all the close tricks — secret tricks — of courtesans, wouldn't you hearken to such a fellow?" Moll Cutpurse asked.

"Yes," Lord Noland said.

Moll Cutpurse said:

"And here, being come from Venice, to a very dear friend who were to travel thither, you would proclaim your knowledge in those villainies to save your friend from their quick and lively danger.

"Must you have a black, ill name because you know ill things?"

Learning about ill things made author Maya Angelou decide not to become involved with heavy narcotics in her life. A friend of hers named Troubadour

Martin was a heroin user, and he let her see the lifestyle. She watched as he and his friends shot heroin into their veins, and then he told her to stay away from heavy narcotics. She did, and she credited her choice to his generosity in revealing this truly bad lifestyle to her.

Moll Cutpurse continued:

"In good truth, my lord, I am made 'Moll Cutpurse' so.

"How many are whores in small ruffs and still, quiet looks — in demure clothing and appearance!"

Puritans wore small ruffs.

Moll Cutpurse continued:

"How many are chaste people whose names fill slander's books!

"If all men were cuckolds, whom gallants in their scorns call so, we would not be able to walk without being gored by horns.

"Perhaps because of my mad, wild, eccentric goings-on, some people reprove me.

"I please myself and I don't care who else loves me."

"A brave mind, Moll, indeed," someone said.

"Come, my lord, shall we go to the ordinary?" Sir Thomas Long asked.

"Aye, it is surely noon," Lord Noland said.

Moll Cutpurse said to Lord Noland:

"My good lord, don't let my name and reputation condemn me to you or to the world.

"A fencer I hope and trust may be called a coward: Is he a coward because he is called that?

"If all who have ill names in London were to be whipped and to pay but twelvepence apiece to the beadle, I would rather have his office than a constable's."

In normal circumstances, a constable was paid better than a beadle.

A proverb stated, "He who has an ill name is half-hanged."

"So would I, Captain Moll," Jack Dapper said. "It would be a sweet, tickling office, indeed."

"Tickling" means "pleasant" here, but it can mean being arrested or being whipped.

They exited.

Sir Alexander Wengrave, Goshawk, Greenwit, and others talked together in a room in Sir Alexander's house.

Sir Alexander thought that his son, Sebastian, and Moll Cutpurse were either married or soon would be married.

"My son marry a thief, that impudent girl, whom all the world stick their worst eyes upon!" Sir Alexander said.

"How will your care prevent it?" Greenwit asked.

"It is impossible to prevent it," Goshawk said. "They marry secretly; they're gone, but no one knows whither."

Sir Alexander was trying to find out where Sebastian and Moll Cutpurse had gone together.

Sir Alexander said:

"Oh, gentlemen, when has a father's heart-strings held out so long from breaking?"

A servant entered the room, and Sir Alexander asked:

"Now what is the news, sir?"

"They were met upon the water an hour ago, sir, putting in towards the Sluice," the servant said.

The Sluice is an embankment that was built to keep the Thames River from flooding the low-lying district of Lambeth Marsh. Passengers disembarked from boats there.

The servant exited.

"The Sluice?" Sir Alexander said. "Come, gentlemen, it is Lambeth that works against us."

Lambeth was a place where many thieves congregated. It was also a place where sexual assignations were kept.

"And that Lambeth joins more mad matches than your six wet towns between that and Windsor Bridge, where fares lie soaking wet," Greenwit said.

"Mad matches" are marriages that parents disapprove of.

Runaway lovers could go to a wet town — a town on the river — and marry.

"Soaking" is done in hot baths as a treatment for syphilis.

"Don't delay, sweet gentlemen," Sir Alexander said. "Let's go to Blackfriars! We'll take a pair of oars — a boat — and go after them."

A landing stage was at Blackfriars.

Trapdoor entered the scene and said, "Your son and that bold masculine ramp — that tomboy — my mistress, are landed now at Tower."

This was the Tower Wharf, the landing stage of the Tower of London.

"What!" Sir Alexander said. "At Tower?"

"I heard it just now reported," Trapdoor said.

Trapdoor exited.

"Which way, gentlemen, shall I bestow my care?" Sir Alexander said. "I'm drawn in pieces between deceit and shame."

Lambeth was a place of deceit because criminals congregated there and because young lovers deceived their parents so the young lovers could get married there.

Blackfriars was a place of deceit because it had a theater where actors pretended to be people who were not themselves. According to the Puritans, theaters were also places of shame.

The Tower of London was a place of shame because many famous traitors were imprisoned there over the centuries.

Blackfriars is in between the Tower and Lambeth. Once Sir Alexander was at Blackfriars, which way should he go?

Sir Guy Fitzallard, the father of Mary Fitzallard, whom Sebastian wanted to marry, entered the scene. Sir Alexander had objected to the match between Sebastian and Mary for no good reason.

Sir Guy Fitzallard wanted to torment Sir Alexander, whose son could have married Mary instead of Moll.

"Sir Alexander, you're well met and most rightly served," Sir Guy Fitzallard said. "My daughter was a scorn — an object of contempt — to you."

"Don't say that, sir," Sir Alexander said.

Full of sarcasm, Sir Guy Fitzallard said:

"My daughter is a very abject — that is, worthless — she: a poor gentlewoman. Your house would have been dishonored if your son had married my daughter.

"I give you joy, sir, of your son's gaskin-bride. I wish you happiness on account of your son's new bride."

A gaskin-bride is a bride who wears gaskins: knee-breeches.

Men wore knee-breeches.

That bride was Moll Cutpurse.

Full of sarcasm, Sir Guy Fitzallard continued:

"You'll be a grandfather shortly to a fine crew of roaring sons and daughters. It will help to stock the suburbs surpassingly well, sir."

The suburbs contained many brothels and were filled with many rogues. The marriage of Sebastian and Moll Cutpurse would result in stocking the suburbs with low-lifes surpassingly well.

Aware of Sir Guy's sarcasm, Sir Alexander said:

"Oh, don't play with the miseries of my heart!

"Wounds should be dressed and healed, not vexed or left wide open to the anguish of the patient, and scornful air let in. Rather let pity and advice charitably help to refresh — to heal — them."

Sir Guy Fitzallard said:

"Who'd place his charity so unworthily like one who gives alms to a cursing beggar?

"If I had found just one spark of goodness in you toward my deserving child, who then grew fond of your son's virtues, I would have eased and comforted you now.

"But I perceive that both fire of youth and fire of goodness are raked up and smothered in the ashes of your age, else no such shame as Sebastian's marriage to Moll Cutpurse would have come near your house, nor such ignoble sorrow touch your heart."

"If you can't help me on account of my worth and desert, then assist me for pity's sake," Sir Alexander said.

Greenwit said:

"You urge a thing past sense; your request for help doesn't make sense. How can he help you?

"All his assistance is as frail as ours, and fully as uncertain.

"Where's the place that holds them? Where are Sebastian and Moll?

"One person brings us water-news of Sebastian and Moll heading toward the Sluice; then another person comes with a full-charged mouth, like a culverin's — a large cannon's — voice, and he reports they have landed at the Tower.

"Whose sounds are truest?"

Goshawk said to Sir Guy:

"In vain you 'flatter' him."

By "flatter," he ironically meant "torment him by complimenting him on the marriage of his son to Moll Cutpurse."

Goshawk then began to say:

"Sir Alexander —"

Misunderstanding "flatter" as having its usual meaning, Sir Guy Fitzallard interrupted: "I flatter him! Gentlemen, you wrong me grossly."

Greenwit said quietly to Goshawk, "He does it well, indeed."

Greenwit was complimenting Sir Guy's torment of Sir Alexander: his "flattery."

Sir Guy Fitzallard said, "News of Tower or of water are both false. They have taken no such way yet."

"Oh, strange!" Sir Alexander said. "Do you hear this, gentlemen: yet more plunges — more dilemmas and crises?"

Things were worse than ever. If Sebastian and Moll Cutpurse were not at the Tower or Lambeth or a town along the Thames, then they could be anywhere else.

"They are nearer than you think thou are, yet more close — more hidden — than if they were further off," Sir Guy Fitzallard said.

He was hinting that he knew where Sebastian and Moll Cutpurse were.

"How I am lost in these distractions and confusions!" Sir Alexander said.

Sir Guy Fitzallard said:

"For your speeches, gentlemen, in taxing and reproving me for rashness, before you all I will engage — wager — my estate to half his — Sir Alexander's — wealth."

Sir Alexander may not have wanted his son to marry Sir Guy's daughter because Sir Guy wasn't wealthy enough. Sir Alexander may be twice as wealthy as Sir Guy.

Sir Guy continued:

"Nay, I will engage — wager — my estate to his son's revenues, which are less, and yet nothing at all until they come from him — Sir Alexander — that I could, if my will — my purpose and desire — stuck to my power, prevent this marriage yet, and banish her — Moll Cutpurse — forever from his thoughts, much more his arms."

The others had criticized Sir Guy for tormenting Sir Alexander.

Sir Guy was betting all of his estate against the revenues of Sir Alexander's son, Sebastian. (If Sebastian were to marry Sir Guy's daughter, Mary, she would be enjoying Sebastian's revenues and later his inheritance with him.) He was betting that he could stop the marriage of Sebastian to Moll Cutpurse if he wanted to.

Sir Alexander could make him willing to stop the marriage by restoring Sebastian's inheritance and income and by allowing Sebastian to marry Sir Guy's daughter: Mary.

"Don't slack this goodness and hold it back, although you heap upon me mountains of malice and revenge hereafter," Sir Alexander said. "I'd willingly resign half my estate to him — Sir Guy — as long as he — Sebastian — would marry the meanest drudge I hire."

"The meanest drudge I hire" is the lowliest maidservant who works for him.

"Sir Guy talks impossibilities, and you, Sir Alexander, believe them," Greenwit said.

Sir Guy said:

"I talk no more than I know how to finish. My fortunes else are his who dares stake — wager — with me.

"I love and pity Sebastian, the poor young gentleman, and to keep shame from him, because the spring of his affection belonged first to my daughter until Sir Alexander's frown blasted all, I would just estate him — let him inherit and get legal title — in those possessions that your love and care once pointed out and designated for him. Once he has those possessions, Sebastian may have room to entertain fortunes of noble birth and marry a gentlewoman, where now his desperate wants and needs cast him upon Moll Cutpurse."

Sir Guy wanted to help Sebastian get the estate that Sir Alexander had promised to him before Sir Alexander decided not to allow Sebastian to marry Mary Fitzallard.

Because Sebastian had been disinherited, the best woman he could marry now was someone like Moll Cutpurse. To attract and marry a gentlewoman, he needed to be financially secure.

Sir Guy Fitzallard continued:

"And if I do not for his own sake chiefly rid him of this disease that now grows on him — the disease that makes him want to marry Moll Cutpurse — I'll forfeit my whole estate before these gentlemen."

"Indeed, but you shall not undertake such matches," Greenwit said. "We'll persuade so much with you."

"Matches" can mean 1) wagers, and 2) marriage matches.

Sir Alexander said:

"Here's my ring. He will believe this token."

Sir Guy would show the ring to Sebastian, who would recognize it and know that Sir Guy was bringing a genuine message from Sir Alexander.

Sir Alexander continued:

"Before these gentlemen who will serve as witnesses, I will confirm it fully.

"All those lands my first love allotted Sebastian — my fatherly love — he shall immediately possess in that refusal to marry Moll."

When Sebastian was engaged to marry Mary, Sir Alexander had promised to give him lands. Now, Sir Alexander was saying that he would keep that promise if Sebastian did not marry Moll Cutpurse.

Sir Guy said, "If I don't change it — don't change whom Sebastian marries — then change me into a beggar."

"Are you mad, sir?" Greenwit asked.

"It is done," Sir Guy said. "It's a deal."

"Will you undo and ruin yourself by doing this, and will you show a prodigal and extravagant trick in your old days?" Goshawk asked.

"It is a match, gentlemen," Sir Alexander said. "It is a wager."

"Aye, aye, sir, aye," Sir Guy said. "I ask no favor, trust to you for none. My hope rests in the goodness of your son."

Sir Guy Fitzallard exited.

Greenwit whispered to Goshawk, "He holds it up well yet. Sir Guy keeps going —"

Goshawk whispered back, "— in the manner of an old knight, indeed."

They were talking about Sir Guy's actions just now. Readers may be forgiven for thinking that Greenwit was talking about Sir Guy's performance in bed.

"Cursed be the time I laid Sebastian's first love barren, willfully barren, that before this hour would have sprung forth fruits of comfort and of honor!" Sir Alexander said. "My son loved a virtuous gentlewoman."

Moll Cutpurse, dressed in men's clothing, entered the scene.

"By God's life, here's Moll!" Goshawk said.

"Jack?" Greenwit asked Moll.

"How are thou doing, Jack?" Goshawk asked Moll.

"How are thou doing, gallant?" Moll, aka Jack, asked.

"Impudence, where's my son?" Sir Alexander asked.

"Weakness, go look for him," Moll Cutpurse answered.

"Is this your wedding gown?" Sir Alexander asked.

Moll said about Sir Alexander, "The man talks monthly — like a lunatic driven mad by the moon. Get hot broth and a dark chamber for the knight. I see he'll be stark mad at our next meeting."

Eating hot broth and sitting in a dark chamber was a treatment for madness.

Moll exited.

Goshawk said to Sir Alexander:

"Why, sir, take comfort now, there's no such problem as the one that worries you. No priest will marry her, sir, as a woman while that shape's on — while she is dressed in male attire — and it was never known that two men were married and conjoined in one."

In other words: As long as Moll Cutpurse wears men's clothing, no priest will marry her to a man.

Goshawk continued saying to Sir Alexander:

"Your son has made some shift — some trick, and/or some change in partner — to love another."

Sir Alexander said:

"Whoever she is, she has my blessing with her. May they be rich and fruitful, and receive like comfort in their issue — their children — as I take comfort in them.

"He has pleased me now by not marrying this [Moll].

"Through a whole world, he could not choose amiss."

In other words: As long as he chooses to marry any woman but Moll Cutpurse, he will choose correctly.

"I'm glad you are so penitent for your former sin, sir," Greenwit said.

The former sin was not allowing Sebastian and Mary to be married and threatening to disinherit Sebastian.

Goshawk asked, "What if Sebastian should take and marry a wench with her smock-dowry — with no dowry but her smock — no marriage portion with her but her lips and arms?"

Sir Alexander's only known objection against Mary was that her father was not wealthy enough.

Sir Alexander said:

"Why, who will thrive better, sir?

"They have most blessing, although others have more wealth, and they will least repent."

In other words: People who marry for love have the greatest blessing, and they repent — regret — their marriage the least, although others may have greater wealth.

Luke 6:20 states, "*And he lifted up his eyes on his disciples, and said, Blessed be ye poor: for yours is the kingdom of God*" (King James Version).

Sir Alexander continued:

"Many who want [need] most know the most contentment."

A proverb stated, "Who can sing so merry a note as he who cannot change a groat?"

A groat is worth four old pence. The proverb says people who lack four old pence sing merrily.

"What if he would marry a kind youthful sinner?" Greenwit asked.

The sinner could be a sexually promiscuous young woman.

Sir Alexander said:

"Age will quench that.

"Age will quench any offence except theft and drunkenness; nothing but death can wipe those offences away.

"Their sins are green even when their heads are grey."

Many sexual sins can be quenched by age, which causes impotence and wrinkled faces and bodies, but old men and old women can continue to be thieves and alcoholics.

Sir Alexander continued:

"Nay, I don't despair now; my heart's cheered, gentlemen. No face can come unfortunately to me."

In other words: I will accept anyone (except Moll).

A servant entered the scene.

"Now, sir, what is your news?" Sir Alexander asked.

"Your son with his fair bride is near at hand," the servant said.

"May their fortunes be fair!" Sir Alexander said.

Greenwit said, "Now are you resolved and persuaded, sir, that it was never she?"

In other words: Are you completely sure that it was never Moll whom Sebastian ought to marry?

Sir Alexander said:

"I find it in the music of my heart."

A masked woman, who was holding Sebastian's hand, and Sir Guy Fitzallard entered the scene.

Sir Alexander then said:

"See where they come."

Goshawk said, "The bride has a proper lusty presence, sir."

"Lusty" can mean 1) robust and heathy, 2) joyful, 3) attractive, 4) fertile, and 5) sexually lustful.

"Now he has pleased me right," Sir Alexander said. "I always counselled him to choose a goodly, personable creature. Just of her pitch — her height — was my first wife: his mother."

"Before I dare reveal my offence, I kneel for pardon," Sebastian said.

Sir Alexander said:

"My heart gave pardon to thee before thy tongue could ask for it.

"Rise. Thou have raised my joy to greater height than to that seat where grief dejected it and cast it down.

"Both of you are welcome to my love and care forever.

"Don't hide my happiness too long; all's pardoned."

He wanted to see the face of the bride.

Sir Alexander said:

"Here are our friends. Greet her, gentlemen."

They took off the bride's mask.

"By God's heart!" someone said. "Who's this? Moll?"

Yes, the woman dressed like a bride was Moll Cutpurse.

Sir Alexander said, "Oh, my reviving shame! Is it I who must live to be struck blind? Be it the work of sorrow, before age takes it in hand: Let sorrow blind me before old age does!"

Sir Guy said to Sebastian, "Darkness and death! Have you deceived me thus? Did I engage my whole estate for this?"

If Sebastian married Moll, then Sir Guy's entire estate was forfeited to Sir Alexander.

"You asked no favor, and you shall find as little," Sir Alexander said to Sir Guy. "Since my comforts play false with me, I'll be as cruel to thee as grief is cruel to fathers' hearts."

Sir Alexander believed that Sir Guy had lost the bet: Sir Guy had bet that he could prevent a wedding between Sebastian and Moll Cutpurse.

"Why, what's the matter with you, unless too much joy should make your age forgetful?" Moll Cutpurse said to Sir Alexander. "Are you too well, too happy?"

"With a vengeance," Sir Alexander said.

"I think you should be proud of such a daughter-in-law as me," Moll said. "I am as good a man as your son."

"Oh, monstrous impudence!" Sir Alexander said.

Moll Cutpurse said:

"You had no note and distinction before: You were an unremarked — unnoticed — knight.

"Now all the town will take notice of you, and all your enemies will fear you for my sake.

"You may pass where you wish through crowds most thick, and come off bravely with your purse unpicked.

"You do not know the benefits I bring with me.

"No cheat — no cutpurse — dares to work upon you with thumb or knife while you have a roaring girl as your son's wife."

"A devil rampant!" Sir Alexander said.

"Rampant" means "standing on its hind legs." Some coats of arms display a lion rampant.

"If you have so much charity yet to release me of my last rash bargain, then I'll give to you your pledge," Sir Guy said.

Sir Guy was saying that he wanted to return Sir Alexander's ring to him, and he wanted Sir Alexander to agree to call off the wager that they had made. Sir Guy had bet his entire estate that he could stop Sebastian from marrying Moll. Sir Alexander had bet Sebastian's revenues and inheritance.

"No, sir, I stand to it. I'll take advantage, as all mischiefs do upon me," Sir Alexander said.

Sir Alexander was unwilling to break the agreement that he had made earlier. That agreement was to give Sebastian what had been promised to him when he became engaged to Mary and to not disinherit him, provided that Sebastian did not marry Moll Cutpurse.

Sir Guy, who had plotted with Sebastian, Moll, and Mary, said to Sir Alexander:

"Be happy and content."

He added:

"All of you, bear witness all then that the lands are his — Sebastian's — and so contention ends.

"Here comes your son's bride, between two noble friends."

The Lord Noland and Sir Beauteous Ganymede entered the scene with Mary Fitzallard in a wedding dress between them. Following them were some citizens and their wives.

"Now you are gulled and fooled as you would wish to be," Moll Cutpurse said to Sir Alexander. "Thank me for it. I had a forefinger in it."

A forefinger is an important finger. Moll had played a major part in the plot.

"Forgive me, father," Sebastian said. "Although there before your eyes I feigned my sorrow, Mary Fitzallard was always the woman for whom my true love complained and whom my true love wanted."

Sir Alexander said:

"May blessings eternal and the joys of angels begin your peace here to be signed in heaven.

"How short my sleep of sorrow seems now to me compared to this eternity of boundless comforts that finds no lack except utterance and expression! The only things my happiness lacks are the words needed to express it!"

He said to Lord Noland:

"My lord, your role here appears so honorably, so full of ancient, venerable goodness, grace, and worthiness.

"I never took more joy in sight of man than in your comforting, cheering presence now."

Lord Noland said, "Nor do I take more delight in doing grace to virtue than in this worthy gentlewoman, your son's bride, noble Fitzallard's daughter, to whose honor and modest fame — chaste reputation — I vow my service and I am your servant. And so is this knight your servant."

The knight was Sir Beauteous Ganymede.

Sir Alexander replied:

"Your loves and friendships make my joys proud."

He said to a servant:

"Bring forth those deeds of land I carefully made ready."

He said to Sir Guy:

"These deeds, old knight, thy nobleness deserves, joined with thy daughter's virtues, whom I prize now as dearly as that flesh I call my own."

He said to Mary:

"Forgive me, worthy gentlewoman. It was my blindness at fault when I rejected thee. I did not see thee.

"Sorrow and willful rashness grew like films — cataracts — over the eyes of judgment, which are now so clear that I see the brightness of thy worth appear."

A servant fetched the deeds and gave them to Sir Alexander.

Mary said, "May I, in your eyes of judgment, be worthy of duty and love, and may all my wishes have a perfect close."

Sir Alexander replied:

"That tongue can never err, the sound's so sweet."

He then gave the deeds to Sebastian and said to him:

"Here, honest son, receive into thy hands the keys of wealth, possession of those lands that my first care provided: They're thine own. May Heaven give thee a blessing with them.

"The best worldly joys that can come to a man are fertile lands and a fair fruitful bride, of which I hope thou are sped — provided."

Sir Alexander hoped that the lands would give forth good harvests and that Mary would have many children.

"I hope so, too, sir," Sebastian said.

"Father and son, I have done you simple — pure and disinterested — service here," Moll Cutpurse said to Sir Alexander and Sebastian.

She had done a good deed for them.

"For which thou shall not part, Moll, unrequited," Sebastian said.

"Thou are a mad girl, and yet I cannot now condemn thee," Sir Alexander said.

Moll said:

"Condemn me? Indeed, if you should, sir, I'd make you seek out someone to hang in my room — my place. I'd give you the slip at gallows and cozen — cheat — the people of the sight of my being hung."

She then asked Lord Noland:

"Have you heard this jest, my lord?"

"What is it, Jack?" Lord Noland asked.

Moll Cutpurse said:

"He was in fear his son would marry me,

"But he never dreamt that I would never agree."

Moll did not want to marry Sebastian.

"Why?" Lord Noland said. "Thou had a suitor once, Jack. When will thou marry?"

Moll Cutpurse answered:

"Who, I, my lord? I'll tell you when I shall marry, indeed.

"When you shall hear

"Gallants void from sergeants' fear."

[Gallants free of fear of being arrested by sergeants,]

"Honesty and truth unslandered.

"Woman manned but never pandered."

[Women having a husband and having sex but never being pandered.]

"Cheaters booted but not coached."

[Cheaters cured but not wealthy enough to ride in coaches.]

According to the *Oxford English Dictionary*, the verb "booted" means "To make better; to cure, relieve, heal; to remedy."

One "cure" for a cheater is to steal enough that the cheater never needs to cheat again. Moll wanted cheaters to experience a different kind of cure.

Moll continued:

"Vessels older before they're broached."

[Maidenheads older before they are broken.]

[Or: Wine and beer in casks aged more before they are tapped.]

1 Peter 3:7 states, "*Likewise, ye husbands, dwell with them according to knowledge, giving honour unto the wife, as unto the weaker vessel, and as being heirs together of the grace of life; that your prayers be not hindered*" (King James Version).

Moll continued:

"If my mind be then not varied,

"The next day following I'll be married."

Lord Noland said, "This sounds like Doomsday: Judgment Day."

Moll Cutpurse said:

"Then would marriage be best,

"For if I should repent, I would soon be at rest."

A proverb stated, "Marry today and repent tomorrow."

Another proverb stated, "Marry in haste and repent at leisure."

"Repent" means "regret."

If Moll married just before Judgment Day and repented (her sins, or her marriage), she would soon be at rest (in Heaven, or no longer married).

Sir Alexander said to Moll, "In truth, thou are a good wench. I'm sorry now that the opinion I conceived of thee was so hard. Some wrongs I've done to thee."

Trapdoor entered the scene.

Seeing Sir Alexander and Moll reconciled, he said:

"Is the wind there now? Is that the state of affairs now?

"It is time for me to kneel and confess first, for fear it comes too late and I get beaten on my head and my brains feel it."

He knelt and said:

"Upon my paws, I ask you pardon, mistress."

"Pardon?" Moll asked. "For what, sir? What has your rogueship done now?"

Trapdoor answered, "I have been from time to time hired to confound and ruin you by this old gentleman: Sir Alexander."

"What!" Moll said.

She had certainly at least suspected this. It was a reason why she had earlier fired Trapdoor.

Trapdoor said:

"Please forgive him, but if I may counsel you and you were to listen to me, you would never do it: You would never forgive him.

"Many a snare to entrap your worship's life have I laid privily and secretly, chains, watches, jewels, and when he saw nothing could mount you up on the gallows, four hollow-hearted angels he then gave you by which he meant to trap you, and I to save you."

The hollow-hearted angels were the coins with holes in the middle.

One way for Trapdoor to save Moll from being found in possession of the angels would be for Trapdoor to steal them from her. Another way was to tell her now that the angels were a trap.

Sir Alexander said:

"To all which shame and grief in me cry guilty.

"Forgive me.

"Now that I cast the world's eyes from me and look upon thee freely with my own, I see that the most of many wrongs done to thee are cast from the jaws of Envy — malice and ill will — and her followers, and nothing is foul except that mistaken gossip.

"I'll never anymore condemn anyone on the basis of common voice and opinion, for that's the whore that deceives man's opinion, mocks his trust, cheats his love, and makes his heart unjust."

Moll Cutpurse said:

"Here are the angels, gentlemen; they were given to me as a musician. I pursue — I seek — no pity.

"Follow the law, and you can cuck me — put me on the cucking, aka dunking stool — don't spare me.

"Hang up my viol by me, and I don't care."

Sir Alexander said:

"I'm sorry so far that I'll thrice double the angels to make thy wrongs amends.

"Come, worthy friends, my honorable lord, Sir Beauteous Ganymede, and noble Fitzallard, and you kind gentlewomen — the citizens' wives — whose sparkling presence are glories set in marriage, sunbeams of society, for all your loves give luster to my joys.

"The happiness of this day shall be remembered at the return of every smiling spring.

"In my time now the happiness is born, and may no sadness sit on the brows of men upon that day, but just as I am pleased, so may all go away as pleased as I am."

Everyone except Moll exited.

EPILOGUE

Moll Cutpurse said to you, the audience:

"A painter, having drawn with curious and skillful art

"The picture of a woman, every part

"Limned and depicted to the life, hung out the piece to sell.

"People who passed along, viewing it well,

"Gave various verdicts on it: some dispraised

"The hair; some said the eyebrows too high were raised;

"Some hit her over [Some criticized] the lips, misliked their color;

"Some wished her nose were shorter; some, the eyes fuller;

"Others said roses on her cheeks should grow,

"Swearing they looked too pale; others cried no.

"The workman each time fault was found did mend it

"In hope to please all, but this work being ended

"And hung open at stall, it was so vile,

"So monstrous and so ugly, all men did smile

"At the poor painter's folly. Such we doubt [we fear]

"Is this our comedy. Some perhaps do flout [insult]

"The plot, saying, 'It is too thin, too weak, too mean' [too concerned with low-lifes];

"Some for the person [dramatic character] will revile the scene,

"And wonder that a creature of her [Moll's] being

"Should be the subject of a poet, seeing

"In the world's eye none weighs so light [no one is regarded as so worthless]; others look

"For all those base tricks published in a book —"

The book may be *Martin Mark-All, Beadle of Bridewell: His Defence and Answer to the Bellman of London*, a 1610 pamphlet that criticized Thomas Dekker's *The Bellman of London*.

Moll continued:

"— foul as his [the author's] brains they flowed from, of cutpurses,

"Of nips and foists, nasty, obscene, disgusting discourses,

"As full of lies, as empty of worth or wit,

"For any honest ear or eye unfit. And thus,

"If we to every brain that's humorous — that's full of fancies —

"Should fashion [create] scenes, we, like the painter, shall

"In striving to please all please none at all."

A proverb stated, "He who would please all men and himself, too, undertakes what he cannot do."

Another proverb stated, "He who all men will please shall never find ease."

Yet another proverb stated, "It is hard to please all parties."

Moll Cutpurse continued:

"Yet for such faults as either the writers' wit

"Or negligence of the actors do commit,

"Both the writer and the actors crave your pardons; if what both have done

"Cannot full [fully] pay your expectation,

"The Roaring Girl herself some few days hence

"Shall on this stage give larger recompense,"

In other words: The actor who played Moll Cutpurse would soon appear on this stage in another play. (Or Mary Frith, the real-life person on whom Moll Cutpurse was based, soon would appear on this stage.)

Moll Cutpurse continued:

"Which mirth that you may share in she herself does woo you,

"And craves this sign: your hands [applause] to beckon her to you."

APPENDIX A: NOTES
— Elizabethan Betrothals —

For Your Information:

With parental permission, boys are legal to marry at 14, girls at 12, though it is not recommended so early. One comes of age at 21.

Sir Thomas More recommended that girls not marry before 18 and boys not before 22.

In non-noble families, the most common age for marriage is 25-26 for men, about 23 for women. This is because it's best to wait until you can afford a home and children. Also, most apprenticeships don't end until the mid 20s.

Noble families may arrange marriage much earlier. Robert Dudley's sister Katherine, who became the countess of Huntingdon, did go to the altar at age 7, but that was extraordinary.

When the participants are very young, it is principally to secure a dynastic alliance. They generally do not live together as man and wife (by any definition). Often, the bride may go to live with the groom's family to be brought up in domestic management by her mother-in-law.

<u>The Contract</u>

Marriage is a contract that begins with a betrothal.

At a betrothal, the two people join hands. He gives her a ring to be worn on the right hand. It changes to the left at the wedding.

They seal the contract with a kiss, and signatures.

A marriage contract includes provision both for the bride's dowry and for a jointure, or settlement, in cash and property by the husband's family, which guarantees her welfare should her husband die first.

If he breaks the marriage contract without good cause, he has to give back any tokens or gifts received.

Betrothals can be terminated by mutual consent. In certain circumstances, one can withdraw unilaterally if the other is:

* *guilty of heresy or apostasy (conversion or re-conversion to Rome)*

* *guilty of infidelity*

* *seriously disfigured*

* *proved to be previously (and still) married or contracted to marry*

* *guilty of enmity or wickedness or drunkenness*

* *if a long separation has occurred between them*

A proper wedding is based on three things: consent, exchange of tokens (such as the ring) and consummation. It can be annulled only if it is not consummated.

It is luckiest to have the wedding before noon.

Source of Above Information: "Betrothals and Weddings." Life in Elizabethan England. 25 March 2008
http://www.elizabethan.org/compendium/9.html

ANECDOTES

— 2.2 —

The source of the Wilson Mizner anecdote, which is retold in David Bruce's own words, is this book:

John Burke, *Rogue's Progress: The Fabulous Adventures of Wilson Mizner* (New York: G.P. Putnam's Sons, 1975), pp. 94-95, 98-99.

— 3.1 —

The source of the Suzie Quatro anecdote, which is retold in David Bruce's own words, is this *Guardian* article:

Source: Stuart Jeffries, "I'm kinda different." The *Guardian*. 2 August 2007 <http://www.guardian.co.uk/g2/story/0,,2139679,00.html>.

— 4.2 —

The source of the Leeuwenhoek anecdote, which is retold in David Bruce's own words, is this book:

Lisa Yount, *Antoni Van Leeuwenhoek: First to See Microscopic Life* (Springfield, NJ: Enslow Publications, Inc., 1996, pp. 11, 57.

— 5.1 —

The source of the Maya Angelou anecdote, which is retold in David Bruce's own words, is this book:

Source: Elaine Slivinski Lisandrelli, *Maya Angelou: More Than a Poet* (Berkeley Heights, NJ: Enslow Publications, Inc., 1996), pp. 61-62.

— 3.1 —

"Whew" and "Hemp"

According to the *Oxford English Dictionary*, "whew" can mean "To move quickly; to hurry away, depart abruptly (*dialect*) [...]."

According to the *Oxford English Dictionary*, "hemp" can mean "*rare transitive* to halter, to hang."

— 5.1 —

Thomas Dekker wrote a series of pamphlets about various kinds of conmen.

Dekker's *The belman of London Bringing to light the most notorious villanies that are now practised in the kingdome. Profitable for gentlemen, lawyers, merchants, citizens, farmers, masters of housholdes, and all sorts of seruants to mark, and delightfull for all men to reade* is available online here:

https://quod.lib.umich.edu/e/eebo/A20042.0001.001?view=toc

Dekker's *Lanthorne and candle-light. Or, The bell-mans second nights-walke In which he brings to light, a brood of more strange villanies than ener [sic] were till this yeare discouered* is available here:

https://quod.lib.umich.edu/e/eebo/A20046.0001.001?view=toc

— EPILOGUE —

This anecdote makes the same point as Moll's anecdote:

Nasrudin and his son were going to market with their donkey. As Nasrudin led the donkey, his son rode on the donkey's back. They met a man who said, "Look at the boy riding the donkey! He ought to show respect for his father by letting the father ride on the donkey's back." So the son got off the donkey's back and allowed Nasrudin to ride the donkey. Next they met a man who said to Nasrudin, "Your son is too young to walk such a long distance. He, not you, should be riding the donkey." So Nasrudin allowed his son to ride the donkey with him. Next they met a man who said, "You are mistreating that poor donkey by making him carry the two of you. You two should get off the donkey and let him rest." Next they met a man who said, "Why are you two walking beside your donkey? You have a donkey, so why don't at least one of you ride him?" On hearing this, Nasrudin thought, "It's true — you can't please everyone."

The source of the Nasrudin anecdote, which is retold in David Bruce's own words, is this book:

Source: Nejat Muallimoglu, *The Wit and Wisdom of Nasraddin Hodja* (New York: Cynthia Parzych Publishing, Inc., 1986), p. 56.

APPENDIX B: FAIR USE

§ 107. Limitations on exclusive rights: Fair use
　　Release date: 2004-04-30

Notwithstanding the provisions of sections 106 and 106A, the fair use of a copyrighted work, including such use by reproduction in copies or phonorecords or by any other means specified by that section, for purposes such as criticism, comment, news reporting, teaching (including multiple copies for classroom use), scholarship, or research, is not an infringement of copyright. In determining whether the use made of a work in any particular case is a fair use the factors to be considered shall include —

(1) the purpose and character of the use, including whether such use is of a commercial nature or is for nonprofit educational purposes;

(2) the nature of the copyrighted work;

(3) the amount and substantiality of the portion used in relation to the copyrighted work as a whole; and

(4) the effect of the use upon the potential market for or value of the copyrighted work.

The fact that a work is unpublished shall not itself bar a finding of fair use if such finding is made upon consideration of all the above factors.

Source of Fair Use information:

http://www.law.cornell.edu/uscode/17/107.html

APPENDIX C: ABOUT THE AUTHOR

It was a dark and stormy night. Suddenly a cry rang out, and on a hot summer night in 1954, Josephine, wife of Carl Bruce, gave birth to a boy — me. Unfortunately, this young married couple allowed Reuben Saturday, Josephine's brother, to name their first-born. Reuben, aka "The Joker," decided that Bruce was a nice name, so he decided to name me Bruce Bruce. I have gone by my middle name — David — ever since.

Being named Bruce David Bruce hasn't been all bad. Bank tellers remember me very quickly, so I don't often have to show an ID. It can be fun in charades, also. When I was a counselor as a teenager at Camp Echoing Hills in Warsaw, Ohio, a fellow counselor gave the signs for "sounds like" and "two words," then she pointed to a bruise on her leg twice. Bruise Bruise? Oh yeah, Bruce Bruce is the answer!

Uncle Reuben, by the way, gave me a haircut when I was in kindergarten. He cut my hair short and shaved a small bald spot on the back of my head. My mother wouldn't let me go to school until the bald spot grew out again.

Of all my brothers and sisters (six in all), I am the only transplant to Athens, Ohio. I was born in Newark, Ohio, and have lived all around Southeastern Ohio. However, I moved to Athens to go to Ohio University and have never left.

At Ohio U, I never could make up my mind whether to major in English or Philosophy, so I got a bachelor's degree with a double major in both areas, then I added a Master of Arts degree in English and a Master of Arts degree in Philosophy. Yes, I have my MAMA degree.

Currently, and for a long time to come (I eat fruits and veggies), I am spending my retirement writing books such as *Nadia Comaneci: Perfect 10*, *The Funniest People in Comedy*, *Homer's* Iliad: *A Retelling in Prose*, and *William Shakespeare's* Hamlet: *A Retelling in Prose*.

If all goes well, I will publish one or two books a year for the rest of my life. (On the other hand, a good way to make God laugh is to tell Her your plans.)

By the way, my sister Brenda Kennedy writes romances such as *A New Beginning* and *Shattered Dreams*.

APPENDIX D: SOME BOOKS BY DAVID BRUCE

Retellings of a Classic Work of Literature

Arden of Faversham: *A Retelling*

Ben Jonson's The Alchemist: *A Retelling*

Ben Jonson's The Arraignment, or Poetaster: *A Retelling*

Ben Jonson's Bartholomew Fair: *A Retelling*

Ben Jonson's The Case is Altered: *A Retelling*

Ben Jonson's Catiline's Conspiracy: *A Retelling*

Ben Jonson's The Devil is an Ass: *A Retelling*

Ben Jonson's Epicene: *A Retelling*

Ben Jonson's Every Man in His Humor: *A Retelling*

Ben Jonson's Every Man Out of His Humor: *A Retelling*

Ben Jonson's The Fountain of Self-Love, or Cynthia's Revels: *A Retelling*

Ben Jonson's The Magnetic Lady, or Humors Reconciled: *A Retelling*

Ben Jonson's The New Inn, or The Light Heart: *A Retelling*

Ben Jonson's Sejanus' Fall: *A Retelling*

Ben Jonson's The Staple of News: *A Retelling*

Ben Jonson's A Tale of a Tub: *A Retelling*

Ben Jonson's Volpone, or the Fox: *A Retelling*

Christopher Marlowe's Complete Plays: Retellings

Christopher Marlowe's Dido, Queen of Carthage: *A Retelling*

Christopher Marlowe's Doctor Faustus: *Retellings of the 1604 A-Text and of the 1616 B-Text*

Christopher Marlowe's Edward II: *A Retelling*

Christopher Marlowe's The Massacre at Paris: *A Retelling*

Christopher Marlowe's The Rich Jew of Malta: *A Retelling*

Christopher Marlowe's Tamburlaine, Parts 1 and 2: *Retellings*

Dante's Divine Comedy: *A Retelling in Prose*

Dante's Inferno: *A Retelling in Prose*

Dante's Purgatory: *A Retelling in Prose*

Dante's Paradise: *A Retelling in Prose*

The Famous Victories of Henry V: *A Retelling*

From the Iliad *to the* Odyssey: *A Retelling in Prose of Quintus of Smyrna's* Posthomerica

George Chapman, Ben Jonson, and John Marston's Eastward Ho! *A Retelling*

George Peele's The Arraignment of Paris: *A Retelling*

George Peele's The Battle of Alcazar: *A Retelling*

George Peele's David and Bathsheba, and the Tragedy of Absalom: *A Retelling*

George Peele's Edward I: *A Retelling*

George Peele's The Old Wives' Tale: *A Retelling*

George-a-Greene: *A Retelling*

The History of King Leir: A Retelling

Homer's Iliad: *A Retelling in Prose*

Homer's Odyssey: *A Retelling in Prose*

J.W. Gent.'s The Valiant Scot: *A Retelling*

Jason and the Argonauts: A Retelling in Prose of Apollonius of Rhodes' Argonautica

John Ford: Eight Plays Translated into Modern English

John Ford's The Broken Heart: *A Retelling*

John Ford's The Fancies, Chaste and Noble: *A Retelling*

John Ford's The Lady's Trial: *A Retelling*

John Ford's The Lover's Melancholy: *A Retelling*

John Ford's Love's Sacrifice: *A Retelling*

John Ford's Perkin Warbeck: *A Retelling*

John Ford's The Queen: *A Retelling*

John Ford's 'Tis Pity She's a Whore: *A Retelling*

John Lyly's Campaspe: *A Retelling*

John Lyly's Endymion, The Man in the Moon: *A Retelling*

John Lyly's Galatea: *A Retelling*

John Lyly's Love's Metamorphosis: *A Retelling*

John Lyly's Midas: *A Retelling*

John Lyly's Mother Bombie: *A Retelling*

John Lyly's Sappho and Phao: *A Retelling*

John Lyly's The Woman in the Moon: *A Retelling*

John Webster's The White Devil: *A Retelling*

King Edward III: *A Retelling*

Mankind: *A Medieval Morality Play* (A Retelling)

Margaret Cavendish's The Unnatural Tragedy: *A Retelling*

The Merry Devil of Edmonton: *A Retelling*

The Summoning of Everyman: *A Medieval Morality Play* (A Retelling)

Robert Greene's Friar Bacon and Friar Bungay: *A Retelling*

The Taming of a Shrew: *A Retelling*

Tarlton's Jests: A Retelling

Thomas Middleton's A Chaste Maid in Cheapside: *A Retelling*

Thomas Middleton's Women Beware Women: *A Retelling*

Thomas Middleton and Thomas Dekker's The Roaring Girl: *A Retelling*

Thomas Middleton and William Rowley's The Changeling: *A Retelling*

The Trojan War and Its Aftermath: Four Ancient Epic Poems

Virgil's Aeneid: *A Retelling in Prose*

William Shakespeare's 5 Late Romances: Retellings in Prose

William Shakespeare's 10 Histories: Retellings in Prose

William Shakespeare's 11 Tragedies: Retellings in Prose

William Shakespeare's 12 Comedies: Retellings in Prose

William Shakespeare's 38 Plays: Retellings in Prose

William Shakespeare's 1 Henry IV, aka Henry IV, Part 1: A Retelling in Prose

William Shakespeare's 2 Henry IV, aka Henry IV, Part 2: A Retelling in Prose

William Shakespeare's 1 Henry VI, aka Henry VI, Part 1: A Retelling in Prose

William Shakespeare's 2 Henry VI, aka Henry VI, Part 2: A Retelling in Prose

William Shakespeare's 3 Henry VI, aka Henry VI, Part 3: A Retelling in Prose

William Shakespeare's All's Well that Ends Well: A Retelling in Prose

William Shakespeare's Antony and Cleopatra: A Retelling in Prose

William Shakespeare's As You Like It: A Retelling in Prose

William Shakespeare's The Comedy of Errors: A Retelling in Prose

William Shakespeare's Coriolanus: A Retelling in Prose

William Shakespeare's Cymbeline: A Retelling in Prose

William Shakespeare's Hamlet: A Retelling in Prose

William Shakespeare's Henry V: A Retelling in Prose

William Shakespeare's Henry VIII: A Retelling in Prose

William Shakespeare's Julius Caesar: A Retelling in Prose

William Shakespeare's King John: A Retelling in Prose

William Shakespeare's King Lear: A Retelling in Prose

William Shakespeare's Love's Labor's Lost: A Retelling in Prose

William Shakespeare's Macbeth: A Retelling in Prose

William Shakespeare's Measure for Measure: A Retelling in Prose

William Shakespeare's The Merchant of Venice: A Retelling in Prose

William Shakespeare's The Merry Wives of Windsor: A Retelling in Prose

William Shakespeare's A Midsummer Night's Dream: A Retelling in Prose

William Shakespeare's Much Ado About Nothing: A Retelling in Prose

William Shakespeare's Othello: A Retelling in Prose

William Shakespeare's Pericles, Prince of Tyre: A Retelling in Prose

William Shakespeare's Richard II: A Retelling in Prose

William Shakespeare's Richard III: A Retelling in Prose

William Shakespeare's Romeo and Juliet: A Retelling in Prose

William Shakespeare's The Taming of the Shrew: A Retelling in Prose

William Shakespeare's The Tempest: A Retelling in Prose

William Shakespeare's Timon of Athens: A Retelling in Prose

William Shakespeare's Titus Andronicus: A Retelling in Prose

William Shakespeare's Troilus and Cressida: A Retelling in Prose

William Shakespeare's Twelfth Night: A Retelling in Prose

William Shakespeare's The Two Gentlemen of Verona: A Retelling in Prose

William Shakespeare's The Two Noble Kinsmen: A Retelling in Prose

William Shakespeare's The Winter's Tale: A Retelling in Prose

www.ingramcontent.com/pod-product-compliance
Lightning Source LLC
Chambersburg PA
CBHW021159160726
47994CB00001B/277